He came to gradually, only the throbbing pains at the back of his head telling him for sure that he was awake. Lines shook and shifted in front of him and refused to be still or join together in any way that he could understand.

He tried to move his body and realised that he was sitting up. When he went to move again he seemed to be falling forward and there was a moment's shock when he was afraid that he wouldn't be able to push his hands out in front of him and break his fall.

Slowly, it dawned on him that he wasn't going to fall.

The reason he couldn't use his hands was that his arms were tied fast at the back of the chair.

Which was why he wasn't going to fall either.

He didn't think much of it.

He went back into unconsciousness . . .

Also by John J. McLaglen

and published by Corgi Books

Herne the Hunter 22: Wild Blood

John J. McLaglen

CORGI BOOKS

HERNE THE HUNTER 22: WILD BLOOD

A CORGI BOOK 0 552 12276 9

First publication in Great Britain

PRINTING HISTORY
Corgi edition published 1983

This book is set in 10/11 Times

Corgi books are published by Transworld Publishers Ltd.,
Century House, 61-63 Uxbridge Road,
Ealing, London W5 5SA.
Made and printed in Great Britain by
Hunt Barnard Printing Ltd., Aylesbury, Bucks.

For Terry and John —
Adam, Gwen, Alun, Dawn
and all the rest...
        just another little Western.

May 1983

'We're his blood. That's the hell of it.' She stared at me in the mirror with deep, distant eyes. 'I don't want him to die despising his own blood. It was always wild blood, but it wasn't always rotten blood.'

Raymond Chandler: THE BIG SLEEP

Chapter One

The house on Rincon Hill was different from its neighbours
only by being more extravagant. The white balustrade that
skirted the garden was more ornamented; the bays at front
and side jutted out at sharper angles; the spikes that rose
from the roof were taller and more richly patterned; the
shrubs were massed together like guards before the door.
There were six windows at the front, fifteen at the side and
most of them had their shades lowered, their shutters
fastened across. The gravel on the drive crunched under
Herne's boots as he strode.

Herne and the house didn't fit.

He was close to a couple of inches over six foot and he
weighed around two hundred pounds. His shoulders were
broad and his limbs were muscular. His black hair was long
enough to curl up from his collar and was greying at the
temples. The collar itself was clean but far from new —
green cotton that was fraying and faded. He wore a tan
leather vest and tan pants over heeled boots that shone
dully over the scuff marks. A Colt .45 hung from his
gunbelt, its smooth butt close to his right hip. The curled
ends of his fingers almost brushed it as he walked.

The knocker on the door was in the shape of a young
black boy with curly hair and a wide grin.

Almost before he'd used it the heavy, panelled door
swung open and the man standing there was black but he
wasn't grinning. If Herne had expected someone dressed up
in a monkey suit, he was mistaken. The man was almost as
tall as himself and around the same age, which placed him
too close to forty to be comfortable. If his hair had once
been curly there was no way of knowing; his head was
completely bald. He was wearing a loose fitting white shirt

and a pair of black pants that looked like he'd been measured for them.

He looked at Herne as if he'd come to the wrong door. 'You got business here?'

'This Major Russell's place?'

'Yep.'

'Then I got business here.'

The black leaned back from the waist and stared at him hard. 'Who says?'

Herne reached for his back pants pocket and took out a folded envelope and handed it across. He'd decided since it was his first visit to San Francisco in a long time, he'd best not mark it by losing his temper with the hired help. Not yet.

The man read the letter cursorily and pulled his upper lip back over his teeth. He sniffed and gave the letter back. 'I'll tell the major you're here.'

Herne followed him along a hallway of polished wood which opened out onto a circular lobby with doors and a staircase leading off it. There were oil paintings on the walls, most of them military, and tall vases of flowers stood on round rosewood tables. Here the floor was marble.

The black went through one of the doors and closed it behind him.

Herne stood and looked at the bearded figures staring down at him, their expressions unmoving and their medals beginning to fade. It took him a while before he recognised the smell that seemed to pervade the air and finally he realised it was a mixture of polish and must.

'The major's in the billiard room.'

Herne stepped over to the door that had opened and followed the man through two rooms and into a third. At this door, the black stood to one side and nodded Herne through, shutting the door firmly behind him.

The sound echoed the length of the room. The ceiling was high and painted white, the walls were white also and light came from a window at the far end and a kerosene lamp which burned from a bracket above the table's centre. There were low bookcases set against the walls, tables between them, one of which held a decanter and a tray of glasses. There was plenty of space around the sides of the table, space enough for the major to manoeuvre his wheel chair.

'Jedediah Travis Herne?'

The reply, 'Sir,' was off Herne's lips before he could call it back.

'You were prompt.'

'I came as fast as I could. Once I got your letter.'

'I was afraid it wouldn't reach you.'

'Luck.'

'Yes, indeed.'

The major slid his cue onto the table and set his hands against the wheels, setting the chair rolling slowly forward. Herne did his best not to stare at the hands – they were buckled at the centre, the knuckles swollen and purple and the fingers crabbed inwards and bloodless. Each application of pressure to the wheels made him wince with pain.

'Pretty, ain't they?' He lifted them up before his chest and looked at them with scorn. 'Like the rest of me. So damned twisted by rheumatism I can't do the simplest thing without so much difficulty that it almost ceases to be worth doing anything.'

Herne started to say something, stopped; he didn't know what to say that wouldn't sound as empty and hollow as the door echoing down the room.

'This game,' said the major, turning towards the table, 'is about the only damn thing left I can do without having someone to help me. Even then it takes me minutes to line up the damn cue and I still miss the blasted ball more times than not.' A scowl passed over his face. 'But it passes the time a little less slowly . . .'

Herne nodded, waited, felt a whole lot less than comfortable.

'Have a drink, Mister Herne. That's about the only other thing I've got the stomach for. All the rest – riding, shooting, women – they're gone for nothing. Memories.' He shook his head and rolled the chair towards the decanter.

11

'Good Scotch whisky. Damn, if it's about all I can enjoy, I might as well have the best.'

Herne took his glass and watched as the major poured his own close to the brim.

'To the success of your visit!' The major lifted the glass and his hand shook, whisky spilled over his fingers and down onto his lap. If he noticed, he gave no sign.

Herne raised his glass and tasted the Scotch. It was smoother than anything he could remember tasting, warm but with a warmth that was reassuring. It didn't take long for him to realise that it was strong too.

'You seem to have led quite a life since the war.'

'That's been over a long time.'

The major grunted and shook his head, almost with resignation. 'Sometimes I think more's the pity — at least in those days I could function as a man should. But then I think of all those lives that were lost, wasted, more to disease than enemy bullets.' He grunted again. 'Whoever the enemy were. Our own people, our own brothers. You, you managed to fight for both sides, I believe?'

'Circumstances didn't allow me a whole lot of choice.'

The major looked away, drank a little more whisky. He was so still that Herne wondered if he hadn't wandered off into some former time, leaving the spoilt shell of his body behind in the room.

When he spoke again, it was as a surprise. 'Since then you've been living by your gun.'

'It was what they taught me '

'No family.'

'Not for long.'

The major looked at him with narrowed eyes but kept his question stilled.

'You may be lucky there.'

Herne set his glass down on the table and without asking the major poured him another, the decanter almost slipping from his crippled hands.

'I have a family and there are times . . . my wife has been dead these fifteen years. Since before business brought me to the coast.' He shook his head. 'Maybe she had better

12

sense that I ever gave her credit for. God rest her soul. Meanwhile I have two daughters, the eldest is a woman and the youngest behaves as if she were – except when it suits her to be like a child. I've done my best to bring them up according to some standards of decency and good behaviour, but when you're restricted to a wheel chair such things are not easy. Young women are especially mobile whenever they're out of sight. D'you know much about young women, Mister Herne?'

'I did once.'

'Then perhaps you'll know what I mean.'

Herne didn't answer. He had met Louise when she was sixteen, married her at seventeen; before she was twenty-one she had put on the dress she had worn to her wedding and hanged herself in the barn. Memories blur: some memories.

The door stood open, and a light wind had sprung up, making it creak on its hinges. He paused at the entrance, turning and looking around at the land about their spread, knowing that he was seeing it for the last time with that special vision that his wife had brought him. The rising sun glistened off the slopes of white, making his eyes hurt.

Inside, it was very quiet. She had climbed up on a box to do it and then merely stepped silently into eternity. The noose had dug into her neck, leaving an ugly burn, but apart from that she looked very peaceful, hands hanging limply at her sides, a shaft of light gleaming off the gold wedding ring.

And the dress looked pretty. Dark green velvet, with white lace at collar and cuffs. Direct from Paris, France, like the book said.

It was a very pretty dress.

Some stayed clear in the mind, clear to the touch. He swallowed the second shot in one and when Major Russell looked at him enquiringly, Herne looked away.

The major reached for a brass bell beside the decanter and rang it several times. Before the tones had faded, the black was in the room, an envelope in his hand. He gave the envelope to the major, looked at Herne with something close to contempt and went out.

13

'He been with you a long time?'

'Since my wife died. Why d'you ask?'

Herne looked towards the closed door and again he didn't answer.

'You don't like him,' the major said. It was hardly a question.

'Not a lot.'

'Nor do most men. Most women either. It's one of the things that makes him valuable to me. I'm the only person he cares anything about. If he thought you meant me harm, he'd break your neck with his bare hands.'

'He'd try.'

'Don't underestimate him, Mister Herne!'

'I'll be sure not to. But bare hands don't stand up to a gun. Not in any fight I've ever seen.'

The major opened the envelope and took out three pieces of paper. Each one had words and figures, each of the amounts was larger than the one before it. Each was signed with the name Cassie Russell.

'She's the grown up one?'

'If she was I wouldn't have sent for you. Cassie's the youngest; the eldest is called Veronica.'

'And what are they?'

'What they look like. They're gambling debts.'

'It seems like a lot of money.'

'It's not far short of two thousand dollars.'

'And you don't want to see them paid?'

'Would you?'

'I don't know. For one thing, I don't know if they're genuine.'

'Oh, they're real enough. Cassie only likes one thing more than gambling and she's pretty enough not to have to pay for that yet.'

'Then maybe you should pay them.'

'It curdles what blood I've got left to pay that sort of money to a man like Daniels.'

'Daniels?'

'Cord Daniels. He owns a gambling house on Kearney Street. It's illegal in the city but he can afford to pay the police force enough from his profits to ensure that he stays open. And besides he only admits the best customers, nothing that will drag the city's name into the mud. Everyone suspects that the tables are fixed and the cards are marked but no one's ever been able to prove it.

'He's got other interests, too. Like a brothel on the intersection of Grant and Market Street where it'll cost a man twenty-five dollars a time to take one of the whores out of the parlour and up the stairs. He isn't a man to cross and he usually has enough men with him to make sure that nobody as much as tries.'

'Sounds as if your daughter chooses her companions pretty well.'

'You'd have to hide a snake a long way under the rock before Cassie's pretty little hands wouldn't come up with it.'

Herne leaned against the edge of the billiard table and had another look at the pieces of paper, they were all dated inside the last two months, the latest no more than three weeks ago.

'Has he been threatening her at all, trying to force her to pay up?'

Major Russell shook his head. 'He doesn't feel there's any need. He's certain I'll pay up when I've stewed in my juices long enough. He's as good as told Cassie so.'

'And he hasn't stopped her gambling?'

'Why would he? As long as she carries on losing, he stands to make even more out of her. And besides – she's young and pretty.'

'And that's how this Daniels likes his women?'

'You know a man as doesn't?'

The question stung Herne more than perhaps it should. He took a few paces around the table, lifted up the cue and sent the white ball across the table so that it nestled against the white by the bottom cushion.

'What d'you want me to do?'

'See Daniels. Find out if anything's going on between him and my daughter. Anything more than these scraps of paper. If there is I'll have it stopped, I'm not sure how, but

I'll have it stopped.'

'And the money?'

'Tell him I'm not going to pay. Tell him what he's doing is illegal and there's no way in which those i.o.u.s would stand up in court. Tell him if he wants them settled, he'll have to get me up in front of a judge. Maybe then he'll stop Cassie gambling at his place, if he realises he isn't going to make anything out of it.'

He downed his whisky and smoothed his tongue around the white moustache which curled over his upper lip. His eyes were pale and watery and the only time they ever gave a sign of life was when the pain hit them and they burned and flinched. His hands were gripping the arms of the chair as best they could.

'In your letter . . .' Herne began.

'I said I'd pay you five hundred dollars now and another five hundred when everything's settled to my satisfaction. If that doesn't seem enough I . . .'

'It's fine.'

'Good. Lucas will give you the first instalment on the way out. Now, if you'll excuse me I'm going to finish my game and then take a rest. I'm not used to meeting people and doing this much talking and it wears me out.'

Herne nodded and set off towards the door.

'One more thing, Mister Herne.'

'Yeah . . . ?'

'There was a man . . . name of Connors . . . I asked him to find out what he could about Daniels.'

'And . . . ?'

'And they found him floating in the bay. His throat had been cut.'

Lucas was waiting in the marbled lobby with another envelope in his hand; this one was fatter and he passed it over grudgingly. Herne pulled open the flap and thumbed through the bills – there were about enough there to be right.

'The major seems to think you're a man to be trusted.'

The black narrowed his eyes and stretched the fingers of

both hands, cracking the knuckles.

'He also seems to think you're dangerous.'

Lucas continued to stare at him, flexing his fingers all the while.

Herne grinned but there was nothing humorous about it; he jutted his face close enough to Lucas so that he didn't have to speak above a whisper. 'Between you an' me, I don't think you're either. I wouldn't trust you out of my sight and I think you're about as dangerous as a bobcat with its claws pulled and its teeth drawn.'

The lip came back over the teeth and this time there was a tight hissing sound.

Herne laughed and stepped back.

'Don't bother to open the door, I'll find my own way out.'

At the door he looked back and Lucas was still staring at him, hostility showing in the tautness of his body, the rigid expression of his face.

Herne was half way along the drive when a movement behind one of the tall, tapering shrubs made him turn fast, his hand moving automatically to the gun at his hip.

The woman caught her breath and stood looking at him, at his face and then, pointedly, at the pistol in its holster, his fingers tight around the hip, the end of his thumb under the safety thong, ready to flick it clear.

'You always greet a girl that way?'

'That depends.'

'On what?'

'On a lot of things, but jumpin' out from behind bushes'd be one.'

'I'll remember that. Next time I come at you from a bush I'll be certain to do it slow enough that you don't frighten.'

Herne moved his hand from the gun and looked at her. She was tall, maybe two or three inches under six foot, and willowy but it would have been a strong wind that would have blown her away. Her hair was dark and pinned up beneath the brim of her hat. Her face was oval and the mouth was full, the eyes were green and they didn't let go.

There was paint on her finger nails and she had obviously been cultivating them for a long time.

She was wearing a white silk blouse with very little underneath, brown riding breeches and tight-fitting boots.

Herne wondered where she'd left her horse: he wondered a lot of things.

'You've never seen a girl in riding clothes before?'

'Why d'you say that?'

'I don't believe you always stare at women that way.'

'Maybe I was trying to picture you in the saddle.'

'You don't think I'm a good rider?'

'I'm sure you are.'

'You should see me.'

'I'd like to.'

'In the saddle?'

'Where else?'

She smiled and half-turned her head so he could get a better look at the line of her nose and the curve of her mouth. 'I sometimes ride bare back.'

'I'll bet you do.'

'Now don't step too far out of line, or . . .'

'Or what?'

'I might be forced to curb you.'

'Think you could handle it?'

'I've handled some stallions in my time and they haven't been any trouble.'

'I'd hate to spoil your record.'

'You'd like to try?'

Herne grinned. 'I'll think about it.'

'Don't think about it too hard,' she laughed, 'it's supposed to be bad for your health.'

'You look healthy enough.'

'That's because I don't think about anything for very long. I'm a girl who likes to get things done.'

Herne caught a movement at the corner of his eye and turned his head. The black was standing at the top of the short flight of steps outside the front door, staring down at them.

18

The woman followed his gaze and the smile disappeared from her face.

'Don't worry about Lucas. He just likes to stand around and glower at people. He seems to think it scares them.'

'And it doesn't?'

'Not me, it doesn't.'

'Your father seems to think perhaps it should.'

'My father?'

'You are Veronica Russell, aren't you.'

She raised an eyebrow. 'You must be a detective?'

'Not exactly.'

She took a step towards him and silk shimmered over her breasts. 'What are you, Mister . . .'

'Herne, Jed Herne. I'm just a man with a gun on his hip and a mind of his own.'

'And you're for hire?'

'For some things . . . and some people.'

She laughed and the sound was as low as her voice. 'I'll remember that.'

Almost immediately she went serious again. Her fingers came close to touching his arm.

'What did my father hire you for?'

'Who says he did?'

She looked meaningfully at the Colt. 'You don't look as though you came to play billiards, or manipulate his joints.'

'So?'

'So it must be your gun he wants you to use – one way or another.'

Herne shrugged. Lucas was still paying them close attention from the steps. A blackbird perked its head on one side on the grass and dived its yellow beak at a worm.

'It's about Connors, isn't it?'

'You tell me.'

'My father wants you to find his killer.'

'If you say so.'

'Why be coy about it, Mister? After all, it's all in the family. Isn't it?'

'You mean his killer?'

Anger flushed her face and for the first time, she looked ill at ease. She recovered fast but not fast enough for the moment to have passed unnoticed.

'You know I didn't mean that. Everyone knows who killed Connors — who was responsible for his death, anyway.'

Herne shrugged. 'If that's the case, why bother to hire me?'

'Because knowing's one thing and being able to do something about it's another.'

'There's always the law.'

'Get yourself enough money and you're above the law.'

Herne turned his head and looked back towards the house. 'You ain't exactly poor. As a family.'

'And we aren't that rich.'

'Just rich enough to hire me, huh?'

'Sure, you and your gun.'

Herne stepped back and touched his fingers to the underside of his hat brim. 'Good day, ma'am.'

'Cute,' she snapped at him. 'Cowboy manners, too.'

Herne gave her one last look from the end of the drive, standing there without a bead of sweat on her body, without a fold of her white silk blouse out of place. Back of her, Lucas' bald head shone almost as much as his dark eyes glared.

Chapter Two

Herne had a room in a small hotel on Stockton Street, near Broadway. It was a brick-built place, five storeys high with half a dozen rooms to each floor. There was a dining room and a bar on the ground floor, a coach house and stable through the courtyard out back. The room itself was large enough for a fair-sized bed, a couple of chairs, a wash stand, a wardrobe and a chest of drawers.

Herne pulled off his vest, stripped off his shirt and poured water from the rose-patterned jug into the bowl. He washed and dried himself on a towel with the hotel's name embroidered on the top corner.

He hadn't been in the city more than a day and already he felt hemmed in, enclosed. The air didn't seem as easy to breathe. Everywhere he looked there were buildings without a break. Even from higher up Broadway, where it was possible to get a view of the bay, he was still surrounded by buildings that were taller than any he'd seen save for his one, dismal trip to New York.

Herne sat on the corner of the bed and stripped his Colt, cleaning it carefully and setting each piece down on the bed cover with care. Only when he was satisfied the task was properly done, did he reassemble the weapon. He stood and slipped the Colt down into its holster, making several practice draws, turning at the same time and drawing the hammer back with his thumb, finger against the trigger.

That done, he reached inside his right boot and drew a bayonet from the sheath that was hidden there. It was his one souvenir of the War Between the States, honed to a razor sharp edge and balanced so that he could use it in hand-to-hand fighting or as an accurate throwing weapon over distances of up to twenty feet.

He replaced the blade, put on a clean but creased shirt and took his worn leather jacket from the wardrobe.

The dining room was full and anyway he didn't think too much of the prices. Down the street and right there was a small restaurant with steam on the windows and a fair-sized crowd inside. Herne found himself a table near the back where he didn't have to share and he could still watch the door.

When the waitress came he ordered steak and potatoes with a side order of tomatoes. It was good and well-cooked, if not exactly the size he was used to. The fruit pie more that made up for that, even if he couldn't have named all the fruit that was crammed inside. He washed it down with two cups of coffee, got a smile from the waitress and was pleased enough by the change he slipped back into his pocket.

From there it was a short walk to Kearney Street.

Gas lamps set at intervals cast a yellowish light on the paving stones and the people Herne passed looked as if they were either suffering from jaundice or had come from Chinatown – which some of them had.

He had some difficulty in picking out which of the houses was the premises Daniels used as a gambling establishment; the streets were not yet all that crowded and no one of the places seemed better frequented than the others. As he waited, it became clear that there were several coaches coming to a halt up on the left hand side of Kearney Street, letting out their passengers in front of a three-storey building with iron shutters across the front windows, an iron gate at the end of the short path which led to the front door. They were men in the main, wearing evening dress and giving the impression of wealth and respectability. Herne watched as the lamp at the door showed them ringing a bell and then waiting patiently to be admitted. In some cases, entrance was immediate, in others there was a pause while questions were asked, in a very few the caller was turned away and walked, disgruntled, back along the path.

Herne set his flat-brimmed stetson at an angle and

walked determinedly towards the gate.

As soon as he rang the bell, the central section of one of the door panels swung back and a face peered at him from semi-darkness.

Herne opened his mouth to speak but the panel was pushed back into place.

Nothing more happened.

Herne looked around at a carriage drawn by two black horses passing slowly along the street, a woman's face palely looking out. He rang the bell again, hammering his fist against the door at the same time.

Again the panel opened; again it closed; nothing.

His hand was on the bell push when he heard a sound off to the right and spun fast. Two men were coming towards him through the shadow of the bushes. One was small, around five six or seven, an equally small pistol held low by his side. The second man more than made up for him. He had to be five inches above six foot and he would have turned the scale close to three hundred pounds. His face suggested that he had a good deal of Chinese blood in him, possibly a trace of Negro also. Instead of a hat he had a white handkerchief knotted round his head. His mouth opened to reveal the glint of gold teeth at the front; a gold earring hung from his right ear. In his hand he held a club the length and size of a normal man's arm.

Herne took a pace backwards and pushed back the flap of his leather coat to reveal the Colt .45 at his hip.

At the sight of it the men stopped.

The big man tapped the end of the club into the palm of his hand.

'Persistent, ain't you?' The small man's voice was high-pitched, with a tinge of an accent Herne recognised as Irish.

'I don't like the door bein' shut in my face.'

'It was never that,' said the man with a quick, nervous laugh, 'for it was never opened.'

'What do you want?' asked the big man.

'What does anybody want comin' here? I've got money in my pocket – that's enough, ain't it?'

'Not for the likes of you,' said the Irishman. 'Take your

money somewheres else. This place ain't for you . . .' He laughed again. ' . . . nor for me neither. Why don't you try down towards the waterfront?'

Herne stared at him, his hand close enough now to the butt of his Colt that his fingers could have straightened and touched it.

'I came here.'

'Sure, an' you can leave as easy.'

'Without a reason?'

The Irishman glanced at the little gun in his hand. 'Maybe this is reason enough. Or maybe the way you're dressed. We only admit the best of society here and, mister, if that's what you are your clothes don't do you justice.'

'I thought it was my money you were interested in, not what I'm wearing?'

'Ah, but generally the finer the cloth, the fatter the wallet.'

The big man was starting to look restless. 'Quinlan, you talk too much. Let's throw this cowboy outta here.'

'Well, now, that's an interesting proposition. An interesting proposition indeed.' The Irishman looked Herne up and down, as if weighing up his chances.

As he was doing this a carriage drew up beside the gate and a tall woman got out wearing a fur cape over her shoulders, the skirt of her long blue dress brushing the ground as she walked. The two men hesitated and then took a couple of steps back towards the bushes, allowing her to pass between Herne and themselves.

'Why, Mister Herne,' exclaimed Veronica Russell with a pointed look at the hand that was close to the Colt, 'you're not threatening somebody again?'

She turned towards the two men by the bushes and tutted. 'Boys, you aren't being unpleasant to Mister Herne now, are you?'

The big man scowled but Quinlan gave his nervous laugh and said: 'Not at all, Miss Russell. Not at all. Is he a friend of yours then, is that it? We didn't know that, did we, eh?'

The big man grunted.

'We didn't know that at all.'

'That's all right then,' said Veronica, 'as long as it was no more than a misunderstanding.'

And she slipped her arm through Herne's and moved him towards the door.

'The gentleman is with you then, Miss Russell?'

'Quinlan,' she snapped over her shoulder, 'you're becoming very tiresome.'

'Yes, ma'am. Yes, indeed, ma'am.'

And the two men disappeared from sight through the bushes and back around the side of the house. Veronica Russell pulled the bell and as soon as her face was seen through the panel, the door was opened and swung back.

They stepped into a dimly lit hallway with a heavy black curtain at the far end. A tallish young man with pock marks on his face made a quick bowing gesture towards Veronica and then looked towards Herne with concern.

'Is this . . .'

'Mister Herne is my guest,' she said a shade abruptly. 'I trust there is no difficulty . . . ?'

The young man shook his head and assured her there was none.

'That's fine then.'

He quickly stepped in front of them and pulled the curtain back at the centre. Herne followed the woman through into a wide room that was fairly crowded with people. There were three faro tables directly ahead and behind them two largeish poker games were in progress. At the rear of the room steps led up to a balcony which held a roulette wheel. To the left there was a bar and on small tables before it a selection of cold meats and cheeses. At either end of the bar were settees and easy chairs, arranged in a semi-circle.

All of the dealers wore white shirts, each one spotless and uncreased. Behind the bar, the two bartenders wore white linen jackets. The two superintendents who walked between the tables were wearing black velvet coats that bulged meaningfully over the left side of their chests.

Cigar smoke clung to the ceiling in a rich blue film.

Herne felt as out of place as a horse thief at a neck-tie party.

'If you can afford to come to a place like this,' said Veronica Russell, 'you can afford to buy me a drink.'

Herne nodded and walked over towards the bar, while she went to one of the settees and waited. He came back with the brandy that she'd asked for and a Jim Beam for himself.

'You always buy a lady a drink so graciously?' she asked, amused by the look on his face.

'Price that feller charged me, I figured I was gettin' the bottle.'

She laughed and took a cigarette from her bag. Almost from nowhere one of the superintendents leaned over her and struck a match to light it for her.

'Good to see you again, Miss Russell,' he said, looked disapprovingly at Herne and went about his business.

'He makes it sound a while since you were here.'

'It is,' she smiled. 'Almost a week.'

'I'm surprised a woman like you doesn't have anythin' better to do with her time.'

'Really?' She arched an eyebrow. 'Surely that isn't a high moral tone you're adopting?'

'Hell, no. I just figured . . .'

'That I'd have some fine-looking man who would take me to dinner and to dances and parties and stuff like that . . . is that what you had in mind?'

'Something like that.'

'Well, Mister Herne, it may not be the same in the Mid-West, or wherever it is you come from, but here in San Francisco there are women who prefer doing things for themselves and not at the beck and call of some man who happens to be holding all the money.'

'Where I come from, as you put it, there's women more stubborn than anything you ever set eyes on. They get by without men givin' 'em a by-your-leave when they has to, bringin' up a handful of kids an' runnin' a farm at the same time. That's a sight more to be proud of than feelin' good just because you can go and throw money away over a faro

26

table without some feller holdin' your hand.'

Veronica leaned back and smiled, shaking her head slowly from side to side, all the while her green eyes fixed on Herne's face. 'That's quite a speech.'

'Ain't it just!' Herne scowled and looked around.

One of the men in dress suits was walking away from a poker game like he was about to pull a gun from his pocket and set it to his head; instead he settled for a stiff drink at the bar.

'Did my father give you money for expenses?'

'Huh?'

'If you have to come here, you have to lose money. I don't see why it should be yours.'

'What makes you think I'm here on your father's business?'

'Aren't you? It hardly seems the kind of place you'd frequent unless you had a reason. And everyone knows Cord Daniels . . .'

She lowered her voice as the superintendent came close.

'If you're going to talk about Connors and what happened to him again, forget it. I'm not interested.'

'Of course you are. Why else would my father . . . ?'

Herne stood up, taking his glass with him. 'Excuse me, Miss Russell. It was nice talking to you.'

She sat and watched him walk between the tables, thinking what a strange, strangely attractive man he was and wondering what on earth he might be interested in if it wasn't what had happened to Dan Connors.

She came up to him again half an hour later. Herne was standing watching the roulette wheel spin and other folk lose their money trying to bet against the house. Veronica slipped her arm through his and whispered: 'Remember you're here as my guest. That means I'm responsible for you.'

She squeezed his arm and he took hold of her fingers and gently but firmly lifted her hand away.

'Don't feel you have to take those responsibilities too seriously.'

27

'A lot of men would give a great deal to have me take them seriously.'

'I bet a lot of men have.'

She leaned away far enough to give her arm room to swing. Herne's hand shot up and caught her wrist just as her fingers were about to strike the side of his face.

People around them caught their breath and turned; the roulette dealer stilled his hand on the wheel. A man in a velvet suit the colour of smoke came through the crowd and stopped close alongside them.

'Something the matter, Miss Russell?'

The look that passed between them was both knowing and hostile.

'Nothing, Mister Daniels.'

'Call me Cord. All my best customers enjoy that privilege.'

'It's a privilege I don't like to earn.'

'Suit yourself. Just do me one favour in future.'

'What's that?'

He looked at Herne as if he was something that had been found floating in the bay. 'Keep your rough trade outside my premises.'

Herne released her hand as a hiss of breath escaped from between Veronica's lips. Cord Daniels folded back into the crowd. The roulette dealer closed the betting and set the wheel in motion.

'Come on,' said Veronica, moving towards the table, 'let's have some fun.'

In a surprisingly short while she had won close to seven hundred dollars and her luck was riding high. Herne tried to persuade her to quit, but the excitement was in her blood now and the green of her eyes shone bright as the chips she was playing with. Herne noticed that as soon as her run took her over the five hundred mark, Daniels reappeared through a door in the wall at the rear of the wheel.

He was a smooth-looking man with brown hair brushed flat and a small moustache that Herne guessed some folk would consider handsome, even elegant. His face was slightly puffed and the veins around his nose were beginning to suggest that his drinking was close to being a problem.

There was a carnation at the button hole of his velvet suit and he had gold rings on the middle fingers of both hands. The hands themselves were large and looked soft.

His belly swelled more than it should against his clothing.

Herne wondered if he wore a gun or if he left that to his hirelings. He also wondered whether he'd do anything to make sure Veronica Russell didn't win too much money, but he seemed to give no sign and she continued to place her bets quickly and without apparent thought, chasing her luck for all it was worth.

Quite a crowd had gathered round now, talking and then holding their breath as the wheel spun. Their excitement when Veronica won again showed the extent to which they felt involved with anyone beating the system.

At eight hundred dollars, Veronica shook her head and said she was not going to bet any more.

Daniels stepped up to the table. 'Why not let the wheel spin once more, Miss Russell? When you're doing so well, you ought to take a chance. You could double what you have there with a single spin of the wheel.'

'And you could win back everything I've won.'

'That's what gambling's about,' he said with a fleshy smile.

'Sure,' she replied, picking up her chips, 'and this is what winning's about. I'm cashing in and leaving. If you've no objections.'

He gestured towards the cashier's desk. 'None whatsoever. I'm glad to see one of my patrons so fortunate.'

'I'll bet you are!'

She gave him one last searching look and moved away, Herne following in her wake. Daniels watched them with interest before going back to his office and signalling as he did so for the game to recommence.

The carriage was waiting down the street and came towards the house as soon as Veronica appeared at the gate. Herne stared up towards the driver's seat, expecting to see the bald head and disapproving gaze of Lucas, but instead it was a fresh-faced youngster with a gap at the front of his teeth and a cheeky expression when he jumped down and opened the carriage door.

'Let us take you to your hotel, Mister Herne.'

'It ain't no trouble, I can walk.'

'And it isn't polite to refuse a lady. Even if you disapprove of her activities.'

Herne shrugged and climbed in, giving the driver the address of the hotel and avoiding the look that came to the lad's eyes.

'My father can't be paying you as much as I thought.'

'Maybe he can't afford any more if he has other things to pay for. I don't imagine you come out of that place ahead too many times.'

'If you're suggesting my father settles my gambling debts, you're mistaken. My mother left me a sizeable sum of money and I draw an allowance from that on top of what I get from my father. I've never asked him for an extra cent and I never shall.'

'How about your sister?'

'Cassie?'

'Sure.'

'What about her?'

'Does she have one of these allowances?'

'Certainly.'

'So your father wouldn't need to pay any debts for her either?'

'Of course not. Why do you ask?'

'Just curious. How the other half lives. That sort of thing. Where I come from there ain't too many women as don't have to work an hour of their natural lives – one way or another.'

She turned her face away from him and looked through the window as the carriage moved slowly along. Herne turned away also, angry with her for her superior manners and her wealth and self-assurance – angry with himself without being clear why.

In the confined space of the carriage, even with the night air coming through the windows, he could not help but smell her perfume or sense the warmth of her. When she shifted in her seat there was a moment when her thigh pushed against his and a jolt went through him as if he'd got too close to a flame.

They stopped and Herne looked out, the lad calling down to tell him they'd arrived.

'Thanks for the ride.'

She didn't bother to look at him, nor to reply. Herne shrugged and jumped out, the driver setting the horses in motion right away. He stood and watched until the lamp that shone at the rear of the carriage was little more than a red dot and just before it disappeared altogether he went quickly into his hotel and climbed to his room.

Chapter Three

Herne woke with a strong feeling that what he'd been told by Major Russell didn't cover the whole bill of goods. He dressed quickly and ate breakfast at the dining rooms round the corner before heading for Rincon Hill.

There was a haze over the sun and mist drifted up from the bay and clung to the branches of trees and the edges of the pavements. It made your face feel sticky and somehow closed and unclean.

The shutters were across and the blinds were down and the house gave the impression of being still asleep — or was that dead?

The little coloured kid was no stranger to Herne's hand.

Lucas scowled from the hallway and asked him what he wanted as if whatever it was he wasn't going to get it.

'I want to see the major.'

'Uh-uh.' The bald head swung from side to side.

'It's important.'

'That don't make no difference.'

'Maybe if I came back later?'

'It still don't make no difference. The major ain't well.'

'He was fine yesterday.'

'He took sick last night.'

'He's seen a doctor?'

'O'course he's seen a doctor. How else you think he'd know he ain't well enough to see folk? He's in bed and restin' and that's all there is to it.'

Herne was about to argue further when he heard a woman's voice from inside the house. For a moment he thought it was Veronica's but he quickly realised it was a couple of octaves higher than hers and figured it might belong to some visiting child.

It was no child – at least, nót the way he'd thought.

She came across the hallway wearing a powder blue robe that was just held together at the centre with a length of cord. Her hair was piled on top of her head in an artistic mess that had likely taken quite some time to arrange and she still had the look of sleep about her. Herne knew without doing so that if he got close enough to her, she'd smell of sleep too.

Lucas turned towards her and gave her one of his best scowls, but all she did was flap her hands at him and giggle.

'Why don't you announce our visitor, Lucas? We ain't never goin' to teach you to do these things properly.'

'He came to see the major, Miss Cassie. An' he's just leavin'.'

'Oh, no. If he can't see the major he can see me. On account of I'm the only member of the family present and receiving callers – my dear sister not having come home yet again last night.'

Herne's mind made a little diversion of its own – if Veronica hadn't driven home in her carriage after dropping him off, where had she gone?'

Lucas continued to look disapproving and as if he'd like nothing better than to slam the door in Herne's face. But Cassie ignored him and invited Herne to come through to the drawing room where she could talk to him and serve him coffee.

'You would like coffee, wouldn't you?'

'Thank you, ma'am, I would.'

'See, Lucas. Tell Ruby to serve coffee in the drawing room.'

And she flounced away like a little girl playing at being grown-up and having callers to visit.

The drawing room smelt of polish like the rest of the house, but the scent of lavender managed to overpower the mustiness Herne had noticed before. Cassie let up the blinds and asked Herne to help her fasten back the shutters and the dull light crowded in on the room as they sat at either end of a long leather settee and looked at one another, waiting for the coffee to arrive.

When it did, Cassie gave a laugh of delight and leaned over for the pot, letting one flap of her robe slide off her knee showing a length of bare leg that ran nearly to the top of her thigh before it became lost in shadow.

Herne did his best not to stare but his best wasn't good enough and Cassie followed the object of his gaze and giggled but did nothing to set the robe to rights.

'You were here yesterday, weren't you?' she said, passing him a cup.

'I was here to see your father.'

'I know. And then you talked to Veronica in the garden.' She pouted. 'No one ever comes to visit me. It isn't fair.'

She sat there looking sorry for herself, a slightly oversize girl whose tea party games weren't working out properly and whose dolls weren't obeying the games she'd set them to play.

Herne wondered how consciously she was playing at being a child herself, or how far it was a role she'd never for some reason grown out of.

'Why did you come and see my father?'

'Business.'

'What kind of business?' she wheedled.

'The private kind.'

Her cup slammed down against its saucer hard enough to spill half of her coffee. Her lower lip jutted out petulantly and her blue eyes sparkled with anger.

'It isn't fair! It isn't! Always business, private business! No one ever thinks I'm grown up enough to be told what's going on!'

She got up from the settee and walked towards the window, the robe spreading out behind her and leaving her legs bare as the cord worked itself looser.

When she turned back towards him, her teeth were biting down into her bottom lip and they were sharp, like the teeth of a small rodent.

'Always the same. Like with Connors. Private business!'

Herne shook his head, set down his cup carefully and stood up. He began to walk towards the door and in a split second her mood and expression changed.

'You're not going! Oh, please don't go. Why, you haven't even finished your coffee yet!'

And once again she was the perfect little pretend-hostess, anxious that her party shouldn't be spoilt. Herne allowed himself to be led back to the settee, the pressure of her small fingers surprisingly firm on his arm, the faint but unmistakeable scent of sleep close about her.

For five minutes she asked questions about where Herne had recently been and he talked to her of Wyoming; she toyed with her cup and nodded and hmmed and when he finished describing one thing she asked about something else.

Her hand was on his arm almost before he realised. 'It was to do with Connors, wasn't it? Why you saw my father?'

'I'd like to see your father now. That's why I came back.'

She shook her head. 'You can't. The doctor was here again. He isn't seeing anyone. Except for Lucas.'

Her face scowled like a child who's just been told she can't stay up with grown-ups.

'Tell me something,' Herne said.

'All right.' She pushed her head back and looked at him, all bright and eager.

'Do you know a man called Daniels?'

'Cord Daniels?'

'That's the one.'

'I've heard of him.'

'Is that all?'

'I've heard Veronica speak of him.'

'But you've never seen him?'

She didn't answer, simply looked at him, her blue eyes widening.

'Never been to that place of his on Kearney Street?'

'What place?'

Herne moved his arm and her hand fell to the smooth surface of the settee. 'Don't play games with me, Cassie. I haven't time.'

He made to stand and she reached out to prevent him. 'If you're not going to talk to me . . .'

'I will!'

'Then tell me about Daniels.'

'I don't like him,' she pouted.

'Then you do know him.'

'I suppose so.'

'And you do go to Kearney Street?'

'Not as often as Veronica.'

'That's not the point.'

'Well perhaps it should be.'

Herne sat back down. 'What if I'm more interested in you?'

She giggled and for a moment he thought she was going to bite her bottom lip again. Instead she wriggled her body towards him and now the robe wasn't covering either leg and Herne couldn't do anything other than look at them and think they were well-shaped and smooth and he wished he knew whether they belonged to a woman or a little girl. He wondered if Cassie knew herself.

'Are you going to tell me about Daniels?'

'I told you. I don't like him.'

'Why not?'

'He isn't nice to me.'

'Does he try?'

Her mouth opened and she hesitated and looked at Herne with a sudden knowingness. She laughed her tinkly laugh, like the cups from a child's tea set being rattled together.

'He tries to be nicer to Veronica.'

'Really?' Herne remembered the scene between them the previous night and found that hard to believe.

'You don't think she'd let him, do you?'

'I don't know.'

'Well, Veronica isn't as wonderful as people think she is. She lets all kinds of people be nice to her. She pretends she isn't interested and walks around with her nose stuck in the air like she's something special and . . .'

Cassie suddenly stood up and moved in front of him, staring down. 'Do you think I'm special?'

'Oh, yes,' said Herne, meaning it, though maybe not in

the way she intended.

'You really do?'

'Sure.'

She giggled and shook her head and then she threw herself in his lap. Her arms came round his neck and he could feel her behind wriggle between his legs and then her mouth was pressed against his and she was kissing him but not like he was Father Christmas. Her lips pushed against him as his head went back and her tongue slid between her sharp little teeth and tried to find its way inside his mouth.

The door opened with a definite click.

Herne twisted his head away and gasped for air.

Lucas was standing just inside the door, an expression of contempt on his face.

Cassie's robe seemed to be everywhere but covering her body.

Herne lifted her up from his lap and set her down beside him on the settee and then he stood up.

Lucas came towards him, another envelope in his hand.

'This was delivered. The major said I was to give it to you.'

He looked at Herne and then down at the girl and something close to revulsion showed in his eyes.

Herne took the envelope and pulled open the flap. The note was brief and to the point and was written in the same hand as the others. It demanded the sum of one thousand dollars, with a reminder that there were substantial sums already owing. It suggested that as an officer and a man of honour, the major had no alternative but to pay.

Herne stuffed the paper back into the envelope and pushed them both down into his pocket. He grunted and went to the door, Lucas before him.

When he turned and looked back into the room Cassie was standing in the middle of the carpet, head on one side, teeth biting down into her bottom lip in a petulant sulk.

Chapter Four

Kearney Street was busy enough with passers-by and people heading for the stores lower down the hill. The outside of Daniels' gambling palace looked no more or less grand than its neighbours, no more or less interesting. Herne went quickly through the gate without the intention of being vetted again at the front door. He went through the bushes around the far side of the house and found a rear door, smaller and without any sliding panels. It wasn't even locked.

He found himself inside a long, narrow corridor which led to steps going down to a cellar and an inside door which opened onto a wide kitchen. A couple of pots were simmering on the stove and there were signs that a couple of people had been eating at the heavy wooden table, but the room itself was empty.

Herne carefully opened the door at the far side and heard the sound of voices further into the house.

He tried to figure out where they were coming from and finally pinned them down as from straight ahead, in the room he thought must be the main gambling room.

After a few moments, the voices stopped and he heard a door shutting. Everywhere else seemed to be still. He flicked the safety thong from the hammer of his Colt and went forward.

After last night the room was strangely empty. The faro tables, the bar, the roulette wheel on the balcony – most of the signs that there had been perhaps a hundred people crowded there had been removed. The surfaces had already been cleaned, glasses and plates removed, the carpet had been swept.

Herne hesitated for a while, waiting for the voices to

return. When they didn't, he crossed between the poker tables and set foot on the stairs. The carpet was deep beneath his boots and swallowed most of the sound he made.

He saw the door behind the wheel through which Daniels had made his appearance. He set his hand to it, knowing that it would be locked and it turned. For a second his breath caught and the skin at the back of his legs went cold.

He turned fast and looked down across the huge, empty room.

The door swung silently open and he went through.

The desk was polished mahogany, papers stacked at neat intervals. Against the left-hand wall a glass-fronted bookcase held leather-bound volumes in unison display. In the opposite corner, behind the desk, a floor safe stood sturdy and solid. Herne pushed the door to at his back and looked round the office again, wondering if there was anything he could make use of while he had the chance. He guessed that Daniels had to keep some kind of ledger, some record of sums of money that were lost and owed.

Quickly he went round to the other side of the desk and began pulling open drawers, feeling through papers and envelopes. He drew out several long, leather-backed books and threw them onto the desk top. Lines of figures, single and double, written neatly in small red or black characters, page after page after page. He ran his finger down the columns, searching the writing alongside for some mention of a name he would recognise — either Cassie or Veronica Russell.

Book after book he saw nothing and his concern about being caught prevented him from proceeding with any real method. If he didn't see what he was looking for in a couple of pages of one ledger, he pushed it aside and searched several pages of the second and so it went on. After a few minutes, he turned away and dropped into a crouch before the safe.

The handle was cold and hard against his hand and refused to budge at his touch.

'Well, now, if it isn't yourself once again. And wasn't I

sayin' you was persistence itself?'

Herne whirled round and found himself staring down the barrel of the Irishman's gun. His hand was close to his own Colt but at that range, even against a small pistol, he knew better than to take a risk.

'Wonderful stuff, this carpet, ain't it. Allows a body to go wherever he wants without bein' heard by a soul. And here's you, caught in the act of robbin' the boss's safe. Tck, tck, tck.' He clicked his tongue against the roof of his mouth and rolled his eyes and motioned with his gun for Herne to stand up.

'Careful now! Be awful careful. We wouldn't be wantin' any accidents, would we? Not before you've had a chance to explain the meanin' of what you're doin' tryin' to get into that safe that don't belong to you.'

He smiled and motioned for Herne to take a couple of steps away from the desk.

'I think we'll be havin' that little beauty you got there by your side,' he said, eyeing the Colt. 'I think you could take her out with the finger an' thumb of your left hand and set her on the desk here. Nice and easy, now. I have to confess I ain't too good with guns myself and my finger just might squeeze a fraction too hard against this trigger and then we don't know what might happen, do we?

'Now be a good feller and do like you're told.'

Herne judged the distance between them, tried to figure out his chances if he sprang forward and tried to dive under the gun, grabbing for his own pistol as he did so.

He didn't think the chances were so good.

He reached across the front of his gunbelt and used the thumb and forefinger of his left hand to lift up the Colt by the grip, then swivel it round, lean forward and set it to rest on the ledgers that were still open on the desk.

'There now, wasn't that the simplest thing you ever done?' The Irishman smiled and waved Herne right back against the wall, so that he was standing alongside the safe. Slowly, he came forward and lifted Herne's Colt from the desk and backed off towards the door again.

'Sure, isn't it a heavy old thing you've got here. I never

could get along with guns like this on account of them bein' too much for a little feller like me to carry. If I had this in my pocket the whole side of me'd be weighed down to the floor and I'd be needin' both hands to lift it up, never mind fire it. But you bein' big like you are I don't suppose you'd have any of that kind of trouble.'

He jerked the gun in his hand and the smile that had been toying with his mouth disappeared. 'Turn around! Now! Fast!'

Herne stood facing the wall as the Irishman came up close behind him. He felt the end of the pistol barrel pushed up against his neck, poking through the strands of hair above his collar. With his other hand, the man started patting him down, searching for some other weapon.

'We don't want to deliver you over to the boss and find you've got some little toy hidden away, do we? That wouldn't make it look as if we'd done our job well at all.'

The hand moved around his waist, up both sides of his shirt, finally along and between his legs.

'That's all right, then. Now we can see what Mister Daniels has in mind for burglars and sneak-thieves and the like.'

He stepped back fast, drawing the gun away from Herne's head. Herne had been waiting for the moment, the second when the metal would no longer be pressed against him. He ducked and turned in the same movement, throwing out his left arm and diving forward.

The Irishman's finger jerked the trigger and a bullet tore through some fancy scrollwork near the edge of the ceiling.

Herne's head caught the Irishman below the jaw and snapped his head back, the force of his charge driving him against the desk and wheeling it round sharply. Herne threw a left-handed punch that clipped the Irishman's shoulder and jumped over his sprawling legs.

The little man went down awkwardly, kicking up with his right leg as he fell.

The leg tangled itself between Herne's and he stumbled, flailed his arms, finally lost his balance and crashed to the floor, rolling towards the door.

The Irishman recovered himself more quickly than he might. He was back on his feet and his own gun had gone skidding across the carpet, but Herne's Colt was still in his belt.

He leaned sideways against the desk and set both hands to the butt, lifting the pistol up.

Herne pushed himself up onto one knee, glanced at the Irishman, turned towards the door. A pair of legs all but blocked the way. His head started to arch back and something heavy came down hard to meet it.

Herne's mouth opened to an involuntary shout and he grabbed upwards and caught air. He had a blurred image of a giant shape bearing down on him, a voice echoed through his brain and whatever had hit him before hit him again.

He melted into the carpet, splinters of light fragmenting behind his eyes for no more than seconds before a warm darkness enfolded everything.

He came to gradually, only the throbbing pains at the back of his head telling him for sure that he was awake. Lines shook and shifted in front of him and refused to be still or join together in any way that he could understand.

He tried to move his body and realised that he was sitting up. When he went to move again he seemed to be falling forward and there was a moment's shock when he was afraid that he wouldn't be able to push his hands out in front of him and break his fall.

Slowly, it dawned on him that he wasn't going to fall.

The reason he couldn't use his hands was that his arms were tied fast at the back of the chair.

Which was why he wasn't going to fall either.

He didn't think much of it.

He went back into unconsciousness.

When he came round again his head ached instead of throbbed and there was a swelling at the back of his head the size of a large egg. Blood matted his hair. His eyes opened slowly, closed, opened again to stare down the barrel of the Irishman's gun.

Quinlan grinned at him and winked mischievously, moving the gun a shade to ensure that Herne had focused on it correctly.

'There was a time when I thought you might not be comin' round at all, but then I says to meself, he's made of harder stuff than that. He'll be back with us in a little while . . . and sure enough, here you are. Not exactly bright as the first light on the hills in the morning, to be sure, but looking pretty awake anyway.'

Herne glared at him and wriggled his arms, testing that the ropes were still as tightly in place as previously.

Quinlan winked again and got up from his chair; he knocked on the panel of the door and a moment later it opened and the big man came through, followed by Cord Daniels.

Daniels had exchanged his velvet suit for a red shirt and black pants but he didn't look any more at ease. His eyes were red as if he hadn't slept as much as he should and his face seemed more swollen and blotchy than when Herne had seen him the previous night.

He walked right over to Herne and slapped him hard across the face.

Herne's head jerked back and then faced the gambler again, staring at him hard.

'Don't try that again, Daniels!' he said.

Daniel's arm swung and the hand cracked back and forth across Herne's face, each slap echoing sharply in the confines of the high-ceilinged room, the ring at the centre of his hand breaking the skin and drawing blood.

Herne grunted with anger and pushed himself to his feet, taking the chair with him. He dropped his head forward and rushed at Daniels, who jumped to one side and avoided the worst of the attack. Quinlan jumped between them and kicked at one of Herne's legs and he lost balance, falling awkwardly to the floor and numbing his arm.

The big man with the gold earring lifted the chair back onto its legs and Herne with it.

Daniels gestured towards the Irishman. 'Give me the gun.'

Quinlan hesitated, but only for a moment.

Daniels took the pistol in his hand and brought back the hammer; he slowly came close to Herne, close enough to rest the end of the barrel behind his left ear.

'You aren't in a position to threaten anyone. You'd best think on that and think hard. One more stupid move and this little thing'll take a good part of your brains out and spread them all over the wall. You understand that?'

Herne nodded, his head moving against the gun.

'Good. Now let's see if you can remember how to talk.'

He motioned the Irishman over and handed him back the pistol, telling him to stand in the same position, the gun to Herne's head. Daniels went back in front and cracked the knuckles of both hands by flexing them in and out.

Herne wondered if he was meant to be impressed.

He wondered if he'd ever get the chance to get his hands on his own .45, which was sticking up from the big man's belt.

He wondered . . .

'What were you looking for in my office?'

'I came to see you.'

The hand slapped him high on the face and his head jolted against Quinlan's gun.

'Don't mess with me! I haven't the time or the patience to waste with trash like you. Now tell me the truth.'

Herne stared back at him.

'It was.'

This time the hand was lower and Daniel's ring opened a cut at the corner of Herne's mouth.

'You were going through my books, accounts – what for?'

'Maybe I was interested in how come you got so much money.'

'More like you were interested in stealing some.'

'You said I was looking at your books, not your money.'

'Quinlan here says you were trying to get into the safe.'

'That's right,' said the Irish voice, soft at Herne's back.

'You best speak up before I hand you over to the law,' threatened Daniels.

Herne shook his head and then wished he hadn't as the pain throbbed harder.

'You won't do that.'

'No?'

'No. If you were going to hand me over, you'd have done so already.'

'I wouldn't be so certain.'

'You don't want the law coming in here and poking around where it don't concern them.'

Daniels laughed. 'That's all you know, cowboy. I've got half the police force of this town eatin' out of my hand as it is.'

'An' the other half waitin' to bite it off an' spit it out along with the rest of you.'

Daniels moved closer to him and Herne could smell the bourbon on his breath. 'I'm losing patience, cowboy. You better tell me what I want to know. And you're right, I won't waste my time handing you over to the police. You'll wind up floating in the bay with your throat cut.'

'Like you did to Connors?'

Daniels stopped short. The air seemed to leave his body and his face drained of blood. He stared at Herne as if he couldn't believe what he'd just heard. It passed inside a minute but there was no disguising the effect Herne's remark had had on him.

Daniels grabbed hold of the front of Herne's shirt and twisted it tight, pulling him forward.

'What's this about Connors?'

'Way I heard it, he was found the way you said—floating in the bay with the throat cut.'

'Heard from who?'

'It doesn't matter.'

Daniels' twisted harder and Herne couldn't avoid the stink of his breath. 'I say it does.'

'Maybe I heard it from the man he used to work for.'

'Russell.'

'That's right.'

Daniels hesitated a moment and let go Herne's shirt. He backed off and stood staring down, his breath coming uneasily, noisily.

'When you were here with Veronica last night I thought it was one of her jokes. Something she was doing to see how far she could push me without my getting annoyed and losing my temper. I thought you'd looked around the place and come back today to get what you could. But it isn't like that, is it? You're working for him, too, aren't you? Working for Russell.'

'I could be.'

'And he's hired you to do what Connors wasn't man enough to do . . .'

'What was that?'

'Keep those two daughters of his out of trouble.'

Herne didn't answer, simply looked back into his face.

Daniels laughed. 'There isn't any one man can do that. They're far past any kind of taming now. Always have been, I'd guess. There's something wild in their blood that no man's ever going to quench. Sooner the old man gets used to that fact, the sooner he'll quit wasting what's left of his life worryin' over them.'

'Yeah,' said Herne, 'it wouldn't suit your plans too well, would it?'

'What the hell you talking about?'

'If they stayed home nights and worked on their samplers, you wouldn't be able to use them to get at the old man's money.'

Herne held himself tense for the blow, but it never quite came. Instead Daniels contented himself with a lot of glaring and heavy breathing and finally he sent the big man off in search of a bottle.

'Look, cowboy,' he said when he'd given himself a couple of large swallows, 'I run a gambling place. If people want to come in here and lose their money, that's their business. As far as I know anything Russell's daughters lose is theirs, not their father's.'

'Then why the notes?'

'What notes?'

46

'The ones you sent to Russell calling in what you say are gambling debts of Cassie's.'

'That's none of your business.'

'That's what you think.'

'That's what the old man hired you for?'

'Could be.'

'That and not Connors?'

'Why is it everyone around here's so fired-up about what happened to Connors?'

Daniels ignored the question and took another drink. The Irishman was getting tired of keeping the pistol to Herne's head and the barrel was no longer touching his skin.

'Why don't you come out with what you want?' Daniels said, getting as much bluster into his voice as he could.

'Why don't you get these boys of yours to untie me from this chair?'

Daniels snorted with laughter.

''Cause I'm gettin' awful tired of talking while I'm sitting here trussed up like a turkey ready for Thanksgiving.'

Daniels gave it a few moments and a couple of swallows' thought. Finally he nodded towards the big man, who slipped a knife Herne hadn't seen from the back of his belt and cut the ropes. Quinlan's little gun was covering Herne from in front now, far enough away so that Herne couldn't jump him, but close enough to blow a sizeable hole in him.

Herne rubbed his wrists where the ropes had burned into them; touched the lump at the back of his head gingerly, feeling the scab that was forming over the dried blood. The small cuts from Daniels' rings had dried on his face, but he could still taste the blood inside his mouth.

'Okay,' said Daniels, 'let's have it straight.'

'All right. Russell hired me because of the gambling notes you've got on his youngest daughter. He doesn't think they're straight and even if they were, he isn't going to pay them. Right now he ain't feelin' man enough to tell you that himself, so I'm doin' it for him.'

Herne reached carefully into his back pocket, not wanting to panic the Irishman's gun. He drew out the pieces of paper bearing Daniel's initials and opened them out, one over the other. Then he tore them into two and two again and two again. The pieces fluttered down around Cord Daniels' feet.

'What the hell . . . ?' he gaped.

'Way I figure it for now,' said Herne, staring at the gambler hard, 'they weren't never gambling debts at all. I reckon you were just pushing for what you could get. I reckon you got greedy an' thought the old man wouldn't have the strength to fight back but would just pay to get you off his back. Except that it wouldn't have got you off his back, because you would have just got greedier still and bled him white.

'You knew he'd hired Connors before and somehow he'd conveniently got himself killed, so you likely didn't think the old man would try that one again either. Or if he did, there'd be some other convenient accident out on the bay.

'Well, Russell may be old and sick but he still recognises the stink of scum when it gets up his nostrils and he still doesn't like being pushed around by cheap trash dressed up in velvet suits and carnations. And neither do I.'

Herne took a pace forward and Quinlan moved his gun but he didn't fire.

'You've had yourself a nice time working me over, Daniels, you and your boys here and one day I'll settle with you for that. But right now I've had enough of the stink of this place and I'm leavin' but not before I get back what's mine.'

He half turned towards the big man and reached out his hand.

'If the bullets are still in that gun of mine, you can take 'em out before you hand it back, but if you don't give it to me right now then next time I see you I'm goin' to ram it up your ass before I pull the trigger.'

The big man snarled and growled low in his throat. Quinlan laughed and Daniels reached for the bottle.

The big man took the Colt from his belt and ejected the shells, then handed it back to Herne, who slid it down into his holster with a rueful smile.

'One thing,' he turned towards Daniels fast, pointing his finger plumb at the centre of his face 'this business with what you say are Cassie's gambling debts . . . it's over, settled. Don't try it again. Ever.'

And, steadily as he could, trying hard to ignore the pain that reverberated through his body each time one of his boots touched the ground, Herne walked calmly out of the room and closed the door behind him.

Chapter Five

The clerk was leaning back in his chair, head to one side, mouth ajar while a blue-tailed fly buzzed hopefully around it. Coarse snoring sounds spluttered to silence every few moments, then set up again. A long-haired ginger cat sat on the end of the desk, its paws slowly opening and closing on the white paper of the register. Herne went up to the desk and the cat withdrew its claws and looked at him suspiciously, ready to jump away.

Herne reached behind the sleeping clerk and took his key from the peg.

The carpet on the stairs was all but worn through at the edge of the tread, scarred by scores of cigar burns that made a bizarre pattern where none had existed before.

He turned the key but the lock was already free.

Herne stepped back and cleared his holster. One hand on the handle he thumbed back the hammer of the Colt, the triple click unnaturally loud in the stillness of the corridor. Carefully, he eased the door open and the scent of perfume came out on the air.

'Good day, Mister Herne.'

He released the hammer and dropped the gun back into his holster as he went into the room and pushed the door to behind him.

'I suppose it's no good asking you how you got in here?'

'You could ask.'

Herne nodded and stepped over to the window, throwing open the lower section.

'You aren't about to throw me out?'

'Uh-uh. Not yet anyway.'

She raised an eyebrow and glanced towards the bed. 'What did you have in mind?'

'Maybe I should ask you that — you're the one who broke into my room.'

'Hardly broke in.'

'You weren't invited and I guess you didn't stop by to change the sheets.'

'Not exactly.'

'Then why are you here, Miss Russell?'

'Since we're in such intimate surroundings, don't you think you could make it Veronica, Mister Herne?'

'Sure. If you'll throw in with Jed.'

'Jed?' The eyebrow arched up again. 'Is that for Jedediah?'

'Sure is. Jedediah Travis.'

'Well, now we know one another . . .'

Veronica Russell took a couple of steps towards him. She was back in a white blouse and riding breeches, but her hair was loose about her shoulders. Her oval face was smooth and pale and her green eyes held all of their sheen.

'There was some talk of riding . . .'

'I remember.'

'I wondered if you'd like to go with me.'

'Where?'

'Oh, nowhere special. Just out of town. Up into the hills. Except . . .' she reached out a hand towards his face and the tips of her fingers grazed the line of blood that had dried darkly alongside the corner of his mouth. '. . . you don't look very fit for riding right now. What happened?'

'I went to see your friend Daniels.'

'I told you, he's no friend of mine.'

'Well, whatever he is, I went to see him.'

'On business?'

'On your father's business.'

'This Connors thing?'

'Not exactly. Daniels' men got the drop on me and Daniels had some fun slapping me around while I was tied to a chair.'

'That sounds like Daniels,' Veronica snorted. 'I'm just surprised he does it to men — I thought women were more his mark.'

Herne looked at her and held his question back. Instead he said: 'If you'll give me five minutes to wash up, I'll ride with you. It'd do me good to get out of this town for a spell and into some fresh air.'

'Okay. Why don't I go down and see that your horse is saddled?'

'You mean you didn't do that already?'

Veronica smiled at his sarcasm and left the room. Herne had just slipped off his shirt when she came back, her head angled round the door.

'I'll help if you like. That bump on your head looks as though it could use a little attention.'

Herne shook his head. 'It's okay. I'll manage. Why don't you see about the horses.'

She laughed and looked admiringly at his chest and shoulders before slipping from sight. This time Herne waited until he heard her footsteps fading on the stairs before he got on with what he had to do.

The hills were green folds that bunched in close upon one another, the grass rich and full and shifting gently in the east wind. Clumps of oak and birch alternated with patches of scrub and low bushes that were knotted close together. Further inland, the shadows of mountain peaks thrust up against the blue of the sky.

Veronica rode as well as Herne had suspected she would, eager to feel the animal's speed beneath her, quick to dominate if the horse gave the least sign of having a mind of its own.

She led them down into a wedge-shaped valley and galloped along through white and blue flowers, coming to a halt beside a stream that ran down from the hills at the far end.

Herne dropped down beside her and loosened the girth of his horse's harness.

She glanced up at him from where she was crouched by the stream, cold, clear water running through her cupped fingers.

'You know he won't let it go at that, don't you?'

'Daniels?'

'Who else? Quite apart from all that money you've told him he isn't going to get, you've made him look a fool in front of his men, tearing up those notes the way you did. I don't think he's the sort of man who can rest easy with that on his mind.'

Herne nodded: 'I figured that. That's why I reckon to stay around a day or so and take whatever he throws at me. I figure that way I'll be goin' some way towards earnin' what your father's payin' me.'

'Sure. That and finding out who killed Connors.'

'I thought everyone knew who killed Connors.'

The eyebrow came up. 'That's what everyone thinks.'

'You always talk in riddles?'

'No.'

'Prove it.'

'Okay.' She stood close against him and there was still enough of her perfume remaining for Herne to be conscious of it despite the wind and the air. 'Kiss me.'

'Now?'

Her mouth tasted of peppermint and her lips were warm and rarely still. The fingers that clasped his arms, then his neck, then his hair were cold and wet from the stream.

The kiss seemed to go on for a long time.

Finally, she twisted her mouth free and stepped back to arm's length, still holding his shoulders. Her eyes were shining and she was breathing slightly faster.

'I always wanted to kiss a cowboy,' she said.

'An' now you have.'

'Maybe some time I'll want to do it again.'

'Uh-huh. Your sister says you didn't come home last night.'

Veronica pulled her hands away and her face went tight and now her eyes were blazing. 'One kiss and you can ask questions about what I do?'

'No, I . . .'

'That may be the way things work out in Texas, or Wyoming, or wherever it is you come from, but here in the city things are different.'

Herne grinned and gestured around. 'We ain't in the city.'

'You know what I mean.'

'Sure do.'

'Don't poke fun at me!'

'I wouldn't dare,' he said, still smiling.

'And don't listen to what my smart-ass sister says about where I go and what I do.'

'You mean you did go home last night?'

'I mean it's none of her business and it's certainly none of yours.'

Herne nodded. 'That's exactly right. I don't care whose bed you slept in or . . .'

She was fast. He might just about have been able to knock away the hand but he didn't bother; he'd been slapped so many times that day that another one from a good-looking woman wasn't going to make so much difference.

The sound cracked out and Herne touched his cheek lightly where the marks of her fingers were clear upon it.

'You and Daniels should get together . . . you seem to have a lot in common. But then, maybe you already have.'

This time he caught her wrist and twisted it back so that she cried out, but not too much.

'Uh-uh. Once is okay. Like kissing once is okay. Any more than that there has to be a better reason than just seeing what it feels like.'

She glared at him, her nostrils dilated with anger. Herne held on for several moments, before letting go and stepping away at the same time.

'You think those really were gambling debts?'

She stood breathing a little heavily, uncertain at the switch of conversation. 'No,' she said finally. 'I don't know. They could be, but I don't think so.'

'Why not?'

'Cassie doesn't go to Daniels' place all that much. Not as . . .'

'Not as much as you do.'

'Not as much as I do. Gambling's strong with me, but for

Cassie I think it's something she can take or leave. It's a little too . . . too normal for Cassie. Her interests are rather more diverse.'

'Such as?'

'Oh, no. That's something you'll have to find out for yourself. She may tell tales on me but that doesn't mean I'm prepared to do the same thing for her.'

'Not even if it would help her.'

'I sometimes think my little sister is beyond help.'

'Obviously your father doesn't share your view.'

'My father spends most of his time confined to his wheel chair or his bed. He's scarcely in a position to judge what Cassie needs or wants. And if he did know, then like most fathers and their daughters, I doubt if he'd care to provide it.'

'You mean he wouldn't approve?'

'I mean that he'd want to throw her across his knee and give her a good spanking.'

'Maybe he should.'

'Or you should do it for him?'

'Perhaps.'

Veronica shook her head. 'It wouldn't do any good.'

'Why not?'

'She'd probably enjoy it.'

Herne dropped into a crouch and scooped water from the stream, splashing it in his face before drinking. Both of the horses were slaking their thirsts lower down the stream.

'If Daniels isn't trying to get that money to get back what Cassie's lost, what is he doing? I mean, d'you think he's just chancing his arm and trying to get whatever he can out of your father, or do you think . . .?'

But Veronica had lost interest in Herne's questions. She retrieved her horse and climbed into the saddle. Herne shrugged, stood up and joined her.

'I'll race you to the end of the valley!'

'You're on!'

Veronica slapped down at the horse's flanks with her whip and kicked him with her spurs. She was four or five lengths ahead before Herne was chasing after her. A quarter of a mile on they were neck and neck and she was using the whip consistently, while Herne leaned forward and called to his mount, letting her choose her own pace and enjoy the race along the valley floor.

They were still too close to separate and going hard when the first shot sang out.

Veronica wasn't certain what she'd heard, her attentions too firmly on winning. Herne responded more quickly, pulling on the rein and turning the horse away and into an arc which would curve it round to the spot where the shot had come from. He was galloping low in the saddle when a second shot raked over him and then a third.

Whoever it was was using a bunch of oaks for shelter and enjoying themselves with a Winchester.

Herne changed direction again, still heading for the trees.

A slug whistled close by his head and he dropped down at one side of the saddle, drawing his Colt and snapping off a couple of shots from under the horse's neck.

The trees almost upon him, Herne launched himself sideways and rolled quickly, using the momentum of his ride to send him towards cover.

Another couple of shots crashed out, one of them from a pistol, and the bark to Herne's right was torn away from the trunk. He saw a flash of movement back between the trees and aimed for it, his bullet ricocheting away towards the slanting rays of light.

Then there were shouts and the sound of horses – Herne went through the oaks in a zig-zag run.

He broke through at the other side in time to see two riders tearing away towards the next valley, driving their mounts as hard as they could.

He straightened, breathed out slow, reloaded his Colt and slid it back into its holster. Veronica was coming slowly through the trees towards him.

'Are you all right?'

'Fine.'

'Did you get any of them?'

Herne shook his head. 'Uh-uh. An' it ain't worth chasin'

after 'em. Not now.'

'Who were they?'

He looked at her hard. 'I thought you might know.'

'Me?' She rocked backwards as if he'd slapped her, surprise bright in the green of her eyes.

'It was your idea we rode out here, wasn't it?'

'But that doesn't mean . . .'

'No. But someone sure knew where to find us.'

'They could have followed us from town.'

'Maybe,' Herne shrugged, looking unconvinced.

Veronica moved off to one side, her face thoughtful. 'I guess . . . if anyone figured out we were going riding together they might . . . well, I often ride out this way.'

'With anyone in particular?'

'No!'

The answer was a shade too definite, a touch too fast.

'Ever come out here with Daniels?'

'No!'

'Connors?'

'I . . .' She inhaled sharply, realising it was too late to lie. Instead, she turned her back and waited.

Herne moved close behind her. Even in the midst of the clump of oaks, the wind moving through them, the sun slanting down onto the ground, he could smell the same perfume he had recognised in his room. He caught himself staring at the pale skin at the base of her neck where it showed through the folds of dark hair.

When she turned towards him, she turned into his arms.

This time she didn't taste of peppermint but something slightly sour that Herne knew was fear. He wondered if she had had reason to be afraid of whoever had been staked out in the trees, waiting, or if she were frightened of something else. He wondered if she were frightened of himself – and if she was, why?

Her breasts, small and firm pressed against him through the shiny white of her blouse.

'Maybe you should tell me?' he said softly.

'What about?'

'About Connors.'

Abruptly, she pulled herself away and flashed him a look of disgust. She went to her horse, her body tight and angry, her fingers as they clutched the saddle white and tense. Herne didn't move, watched her ride back through the trees without turning her head. He waited for some minutes, turning over in his mind what she'd said – thinking about what she hadn't said at all. Then he turned his attention to the tracks the riders had left in the haste of their flight.

Chapter Six

San Angelo was a small place north east of San Francisco.
Sometime ago there had been a Spanish mission there and
now all that remained to show it was a weather-beaten
adobe church and a tower that was crumbling slow but sure
towards the dust of the flat, wide street. The fixture that had
once held the iron bell was rusted and empty. One wing of
the cross that crowned the church had been broken
off.

A pair of gnarled pepper trees stood guard outside the
arched entrance.

Herne rode up slow, the flat brim of his stetson angled
steeply against the afternoon sun.

A boy with tousled hair and large, brown eyes, scuttled
up from where he'd been sitting in the shadow of the wall
and hurried towards him. He was wearing the loose cotton
shirt and pants of the Mexican *peons*. He was favouring his
left leg, a limp that he was doing his best to disguise.

'*Senor?*'

'Two men rode in here, some time in the last hour . . .'

'*Gringos, senor?*'

Herne shrugged. 'Could be. I don't know. But they been
ridin' pretty hard. Horses'd be all lathered up.'

'What of them, *senor?*'

'They ride on through?'

The boy stared at him for several moments before
shaking his head slowly from side to side.

'Know where they are now?'

Again the pause, and this time the head nodded yes.

'Take me to 'em?'

The eyes widened with concern and there was no answer,
no gesture.

'You don't have to come near. You won't get hurt. Just point 'em out, that's all.'

Still the boy hesitated, his eyes flicking away from Herne towards the small group of buildings to the left.

Herne took a dollar piece from his pocket and flipped it once in the air, catching it and tossing it down between the boy's feet in one movement.

'Come with me.'

He took hold of the horse's bridle and led Herne past half a dozen flat-roofed adobes towards a well that was bricked round where the street widened out. A woman with a scarf around her head paused in hauling her bucket to the top and watched Herne and the boy with concern.

The boy said something to her in Mexican and she finished pulling the water to the surface, freed the bucket, set in on her shoulder and hurried away.

The boy moved to Herne's side, touching the shiny metal of the stirrup, his fingers running back and forth along it, stroking it.

'See there, the store . . .'

Herne looked across at a wooden building, low and flat save for one end where a second floor had been added in a ramshackle way that gave the impression it was going to fall to the ground with the first good wind. Signs scrawled on the wall advertised beer and tequilla, tacos and tortillas. An old curtain hung across one window, a piece of blanket half-covered the other. There were a couple of mangy-looking dogs outside, curled in the dirt on either side of the door, ignoring one another totally.

The door swung open and closed with the wind, creaking each time.

Five horses were tethered to the hitching rail outside.

'They in there?' Herne asked quietly.

'*Si, senor.*'

'An' their mounts . . .?'

'There, *senor*.' The boy pointed to the end of the line, a pinto and a grey. Herne could see the flecks of lather and the dark of sweat still on their coats.

He loosed the safety thong from the hammer of his Colt

and lifted it clear, spinning the chamber and checking the load.

'Know who else is in there?'

The boy shook his head, no.

'Okay.' Herne let the gun fall back to the holster, swung his leg and dropped to the street. He handed the reins to the boy. 'You look out for her. Have her ready case I have to leave in a hurry. You understand me now?'

Excitement lit up the boy's eyes, his face.

'*Si, senor*. I will do this.'

'Good kid.' Herne ruffled the boy's hair, grinned down at him, and began to walk across the square.

A dust ball rolled and skipped in front of him as the heels of his boots pushed crisply into the packed dirt. To his right a door opened and closed and he covered the movement but still kept walking. One of the dogs yawned and nipped absent-mindedly into its sandy coat for fleas.

Herne paused at the end of the rail and bent down, quickly examining the pinto and the grey.

The door creaked back and then banged against its frame.

Herne set the palm of his left hand against it and pushed it open, holding it wide. The fingers of his other hand grazed the butt of his Colt. Eyes narrowed, he peered into the long room.

A couple of trestle tables were arranged at the centre so as to make a wide counter, one of them holding bottles of liquor and glasses, the other laden with small crates and boxes. To the right there was an assortment of larger crates, sacks and more boxes, none of them arranged in any apparent order. Shoes sat alongside flour; nails kept company with fence posts and biscuits; coffee was forced into a gap between bottles of cure-all and boxes of ammunition.

Over to the left there were a few tables and chairs, a couple of bunk beds and a blackened stove with a round-bellied pot of what smelt like chilli simmering inside it.

Herne picked out the two men he was looking for right off.

They were sitting over against the rear window, eating. One had his chair hooked back so that it was balanced on its hind legs, knees resting up against the edge of the table. He had more than a trace of Mex in him, but mostly he was white. His hair was thick with grease and hung in clumps; he had a beard that was tangled and spotted red with the droppings of chilli that hadn't made the distance from plate to mouth.

His companion was younger by ten or more years, not much more than a kid. He was trying to grow a moustache without too much luck, just a grey shadow over his upper lip. He'd turned his head towards the door when Herne had entered and his fork was frozen midway between his face and the tortilla that was getting cold on his plate. He chewed slowly at whatever remained in his mouth, watching.

A couple of Mexicans sat between that pair and the door, playing cards and drinking beer.

A fifth man was stretched out on one of the bunks, one arm over his head the way a cat does to keep out the light. He could have been asleep or he could have been drunk — or simply playing possum. As yet Herne had no way of knowing.

'Howdy, stranger.'

The greeting came from a shrivelled man with silver hair on one side of his head and blotched skin on the other. His face was twisted up at the left side of his mouth and the eye on that side was dead as if maybe it was made out of glass.

He shuffled along behind the counter, one half of his face smiling.

'Passin' through?'

'You could say,' Herne answered, not really looking at the man, looking at the couple over by the grimy window instead.

'Beer?'

'Okay.'

'It's good an' cold.'

'I said, okay.'

The man chewed at the inside of his mouth and opened a

bottle, pushing a glass across the table in Herne's direction.

'Travelled far?'

'Can't say I have. Rode out from town a spell. Hills south of here.'

Herne poured half the beer into the glass, tilting it so that the liquor didn't froth up the glass, tilting his head so that he could see the worried glances being exchanged between the couple at the back of the room.

'Mite warm for ridin' far,' said the silver-haired man.

'Yeah, happen so. Specially when there's folk around wantin' to make it hotter.'

'Come again?'

'Feller sets himself up back of some trees with a Winchester, tries his hand at bushwacking. Only this feller, his hand ain't too good. Don't get it done.'

The breed jolted the table hard as his chair rocked down. His hand disappeared from sight, but the man with him shook his head and leaned across and told him to hold hard.

Silver-hair twisted his head and stared glassily over towards the corner.

'Anyone special you got on your mind?' he asked, turning back towards Herne again.

Herne took another swallow at the beer. Sweat was running down both sides of his face from under the brim of his stetson; more of it caught at the nape of his neck and at his crotch; more ran down his nose and dropped onto the trestle table.

He wiped the palm of his right hand down the leg of his pants.

'There's a pinto outside with a Winchester in the scabbard. A grey that runs heavy on the left side, got a crack across the curve of its rear shoe. That . . .'

He'd said enough.

The breed jumped again and this time the kid made no attempt to hold him.

The breed had a Smith and Wesson .45 with a filed-down trigger and he wasn't slow. Chilli flew into the air as the table leaped upwards and the plate careened across and collided with the kid's tortilla. The breed's chair cracked back against the wall and the barrel of the pistol swung clear of the rocking table edge.

The kid threw himself sideways and dived for the floor.

Herne rocked backwards on his heels and his hand blurred through a fast arc that had Silver-hair staring open-mouthed.

The breed yelled something and squeezed back on the trigger but the sound of his voice was buried in the roar from Herne's Colt and a .45 slug was tearing through his shoulder before his own shot dug into the ceiling high to Herne's left.

'Jesus Christ!' breathed the owner and his mouth stayed open.

One of the Mexicans had time to cross himself; the other wanted to sneak a look at his opponent's cards but didn't have the time.

The breed hit the wall close by the window frame and fell face forward, his nose striking the centre of the table with a crash that broke the cartilege and fractured the bone.

His companion was still on the ground, still watching, waiting, making no move for his own gun.

Herne had the hammer of the Colt back and his arm outstretched, sighting along the barrel.

Slowly the breed pushed himself up from the table, chilli dripping from his face and beard, mingling with the blood that flowed freely from his shattered nose.

The Smith and Wesson was still in his right hand, but his shoulder was screaming with pain and he couldn't have raised his arm if he'd wanted. He grimaced and pain flooded his eyes. Herne could have been little more than a blur across the other side of the room.

He may have been little more than a backshooter who'd sell what little pride he had and take another man's life for a couple of pieces of silver, but something gave him some guts then. Maybe nothing more than the sure and certain knowledge that he was going to die anyway.

He winced and buckled forwards, pushing the Smith and Wesson across the table, clawing for it with his left hand.

'Don't do it!' called Herne.

The fingers fumbled with the grip, twisted it upwards as the man's face contorted with pain. The left side of his shirt was dark with blood. His eyes blinked hard as he tried to steady himself against the wall.

'Don't!'

The pistol kept on coming.

Herne sighed and squeezed back on the trigger.

The breed went back against the wall, his right side thrown round and his arm jolting out and smashing through the filthy, cobwebbed glass. A hole the size of a man's fist had ripped its way through the centre of his chest and the slug had deflected off the breast bone and torn a way through back of his ribs.

Glass splintered about him and the breed fell head first through the gaping pane and slumped over the sill.

'God almighty!' breathed the silver-haired man and inched a fraction closer to the sawn-off he kept stashed between crates on the floor.

The Mexican crossed himself again and mouthed a few anxious prayers.

There were footsteps running in the street outside, but they stopped well short of the door.

Herne angled the Colt round and gestured for the kid to get up from the floor.

He came up good and slow, his tongue wetting his lips nervously, the tip of it grazing the edges of his pitiful little moustache. A boy playing at being a man before his time. Herne recalled himself at fifteen, sixteen: one man's death already back of him and riding for the Pony Express out of Fort Bridger. Him and Bill Cody.

The kid's eyes darted towards the creaking door and Herne knew he was reckoning his chances of reaching one of the broncs outside.

His hand drifted towards the Colt at his belt and Herne knew he was thinking of that also – one lucky shot or going out in a blast of pointless glory.

'You saw what happened to your friend.'

The kid nodded, blinked, nodded. Herne doubted if he

was a day over sixteen.

'Ain't no reason for it to be like that with you.'

'You reckon it was us as tried to bushwack you . . .'

'I know damn well it was!' Herne snarled.

'Then you ain't . . .'

'I ain't goin' to gun you down in cold blood. Save that for the likes of your friend over there.' Herne nodded towards the window.

First one Mexican then the other got up from the table and backed off towards the door, hands clawing the stifling air above their heads.

The man on the bunk groaned in his drunken stupor and wrapped both arms about his head.

'That Winchester . . . it's in his saddle, ain't it?'

The kid nodded.

'Then let's just say you was along for the ride. Which means all you got to do is answer a coupla questions.'

The kid licked his lips all the more and gulped stale air. 'That means . . .'

'That means you can leave your gun an' ride out of here scotfree.'

'You give me . . . your word on that?' the kid stumbled out.

'You got it.'

The kid sighed and his shoulders slumped and he glanced over at the dead man hanging half in and half out of the window, but he wasn't about to interfere.

'Okay,' he said at last. 'Okay, tell me what you want to know. Long as you'll keep your word.'

'I always have.'

'Sure,' the kid nodded, drawing in more air. 'Sure.'

'Who sent you out here?' asked Herne. 'Who paid you to bushwack me? That's the . . .'

Silver-hair was quiet and smooth and for a man whose body wasn't close to the state it had once been, he was pretty fast. Maybe it was accident as much as anything that knocked the end of the sawn-down barrels against the glass as he swung it round – maybe having only one good eye didn't allow him to judge it as he should.

Either way, the sound spun Herne fast and sent him diving for the floor.

Both barrels exploded over his head.

Herne's elbows jarred against the boards and the Colt was jolted from his grasp and spun away out of reach.

He pushed his left hand to the ground and levered himself to his feet, right hand snaking inside his boot for the handle of the hidden bayonet. He sprang onto the nearest of the two trestle tables and it rocked and gave beneath his weight, sending glasses and bottles flying in a torrent of splinters.

Silver-hair swung the shotgun for Herne's head and he ducked underneath it, the end of the barrels raking the back of his head and opening the largest of the scabs he'd picked up the day before.

The impetus of his jump carried him on, under the swing and smack into the owner's frail body.

The two of them accounted for the second table and a welter of boxes and crates bounced around them.

Herne saw the twisted face close to his and jutted his head down fast, butting him between the eyes.

The man's head jolted back hard and before it could swing back the point of Herne's bayonet was resting against his Adam's apple.

The one good eye focused on Herne and blinked while the glass one continued to stare emptily.

The merest trail of blood began to trickle down from his neck.

Herne caught hold of his shirt and lifted him to his feet, keeping the bayonet where it was.

The line of blood thickened.

Herne withdrew the bayonet, pulled the man close to him and pushed him away again fast, his arm jerking straight as a ramrod.

Silver-hair went cannoning from one stack of boxes to another, finally landing in a heap by the side wall.

Herne was over him in a second, dragging him up and tossing him round, pushing him down over one of the collapsed tables.

Silver-hair screamed as the bayonet blade flashed through the air and wet himself as it passed through the collar of his shirt and pinned him to the table top.

Herne shook his head and stepped away. His gun was close by the door and he went over and scooped it up.

Silver-hair was shaking and the room stank like he'd lost control of his bowels along with the rest.

Herne pointed the gun at his head. 'I wondered why they rode here. Now I know. It was to collect the rest of their money.' He grunted. 'What'd they tell you? They'd left me up there in the hills dead? That what they said? They sure as hell didn't ride back here an' tell you they messed up.'

He didn't answer, didn't do anything but stare.

'Who set you up for it?'

The mouth opened but all that emerged was a drool of saliva mixed with blood.

'You know you're goin' to tell me, don't you? One way or another. It'll hurt a whole lot more than it does now if you waste my time.'

Silver-hair's mouth wobbled and he finally spat out: 'I ain't tellin' you. No matter . . . matter what you . . .'

Herne shot him through the right leg, splintering the kneecap to shards of bone.

Silver-hair screamed and reached down for his shattered knee but the bayonet held him fast, the shirt tearing but not enough to come free.

'You'll tell me,' Herne assured him. 'It's just a matter of when. How many bullets.'

'No . . . I . . . won't . . .'

Herne took careful aim at the other leg and began to squeeze back on the trigger.

'All right! All right!'

Herne grinned and released the hammer carefully, dropping the Colt back to his side.

His hand rested on the handle of the bayonet.

'Bellour. His name's Ray Bellour. He's got an office in town.'

'What kind of office?'

'Sort of . . . he paints portraits, society folk mostly.

68

That an' pictures, daguerreotypes. He . . .'

'What's his interest in me?' Herne snarled.

'I don't know. Honest. I don't know. He just paid me to get it done. Any way, he said. Any way.'

'He tell you where I'd be?'

The single eye closed and the silver head nodded.

'Why these two?' Herne asked, nodding across the room.

'They was here. Didn't figure I could ride out myself. I offered 'em half.'

'Half of how much?' asked Herne, wondering how much he was worth dead to a man he'd never seen or heard of.

'Two hundred dollars.'

Herne jerked the bayonet loose and the man collapsed to the floor, grasping his shattered leg and moaning loudly.

Herne went to the cashbox that had been knocked to the floor and turned the key, grabbing a handful of bills that likely came to close on a hundred dollars.

On his way back across the room, he bent over the kid he'd been questioning before Silver-hair had made his move. The shot from the sawn-off had lifted him off his feet and thrown him clear across the room. Small holes peppered his face and chest and his faint line of moustache was tinged with red. He looked even younger than his sixteen years and he wouldn't get any older.

Herne took one final glance at the wreck of a man writhing in his own blood and mess in the middle of the room and pushed his way out into the warm air.

There were a dozen or so people outside and they all backed off as Herne emerged and no one made a move to stop him leaving. The boy was waiting by the well, holding the reins of his horse. Herne dipped the scoop into the bucket of water that rested on the brick surround and drank deep. Then he took the reins and said thanks to the boy, hauling himself into the saddle. At the last moment, he swung down and reached out for the boy's hand and when he pulled away there were close on a hundred dollar bills fluttering between the boy's astonished fingers.

Chapter Seven

A small crowd stood around the liberty pole at the centre of Portsmouth Square, listening to a white-suited politician stomping his feet on the improvised rostrum, thumping his fist into his palm and demanding that the entire Chinese population of California be deported and that San Francisco's Chinatown be burned to the ground forthwith.

Apart from one youth with a wall-eye who fingered a length of timber nervously and yelled approval for the speaker's more violent ideas, nobody seemed about to march off in search of burning brands.

Near the edge of the crowd a Chinaman wearing a skin-tight black cap and loose-fitting black clothes walked slowly round selling food from a tray. He was apparently oblivious to the politician's rhetoric, and the crowd seemed oblivious to him – except when it came to buying spring rolls.

Herne stood some ten yards off from the small crowd, the ground beneath his feet more mud than grass. Half of the trees that had been planted inside the park railings had failed to grow and hardly outshone the wooden stakes which had been driven into the ground to support them; others had clearly been pulled up, perhaps by a mob fired more successfully than the present docile scattering.

So far Herne had seen nothing of the gangs of young hoodlums who were rumoured to live in the city, mostly around the docks, coming out into the streets at night and terrorising anyone foolish enough to walk alone or insufficiently armed. The stories he had heard told of groups of as many as fifty, armed with clubs and knives, razors and occasionally guns; tales of rape and robbery, throats cut and bodies drifting in the bay.

Again his mind went to Connors, trying to fit him into a pattern that seemed to be becoming increasingly difficult to contain.

He took a few paces across the square. Immediately ahead of him was the McLaughlin Mail and Stage Office, connecting with Oakland, San Juan, Santa Cruz and Stockton, onto Sacramento. The road in front of it had been paved with irregular cobbles and a coach stood waiting for departure, one of the team thrusting its head over the park railings and eating the leaves from the beginnings of a tree.

To his left was a sloping street of buildings that were mostly brick, all at least two storeys high. John Piper, Dealer in Fruits; Lanszwtert's Pharmacy and Chemical Laboratory; Lucas Fine: Gun Smith; the Plaza Bakery; the narrow building with a white awning to the right of the bakery had the name Ray Bellour painted in red script above the varnished door.

Herne crossed the street and looked through the window. A painting of a woman holding a small bouquet of flowers was set on an easel at the centre; she was wearing a pale blue dress and there was something Spanish or Mexican about her, apart from the fact that her hair, pulled back and turned into a tight coil, was fair. Several smaller paintings, one of a soldier in uniform, the others of women and children, were arranged at either side. The side wall held a display of daguerreotypes, some of them family portraits, others women posed against a background of lace and ornate furniture.

Herne went next door to the bakery and bought a sweet roll and ate it hungrily; he bought a second and, still licking the sweetness from his fingers, pushed the door open to Bellour's store.

A woman was sitting behind a desk towards the rear of the room, her back as straight as if someone had tied a poker to her spine before leaving her in place.

The heels of Herne's boots sank into the Indian carpet as he walked towards her.

'You'd like to buy a painting, sir? Or maybe you've come

to arrange for a sitting. The rates are . . . '

'I want to see Bellour.'

'Sorry?'

'I said I want to see Bellour.'

It was clear she wasn't used to being talked to that way. Her back couldn't get any straighter, but her neck arched steeply and her eyes became dark pin holes. She was wearing a black suit with a crisp white blouse, her hair was dark and pinned close to her head in a bun. There was deep red paint on her fingernails.

'Mister Bellour is . . . '

The door in the wall behind her opened and a man's head poked out. He was open-faced and sandy-haired and one of his front teeth was cracked across. He started to say something to the woman, saw Herne and thought better of it.

Back of him, Herne could see that there were packages wrapped in brown paper and apparently ready to be moved. He could see daylight through an open back door and the outline of a small delivery wagon.

The door in the wall slammed shut.

The woman at the desk ground her teeth.

'That Bellour?' asked Herne, moving closer.

'Mister Bellour is not on the premises.'

'Then who . . . ?'

'That was Mister Bellour's assistant.'

'Then maybe I'd best speak to him.'

Herne started to go round the desk and the woman pulled open the drawer by her right hand. There was a sharp intake of breath and Herne turned to find himself staring at a Remington-Eliot that sat snug in her hand, one red-nailed finger resting against the unguarded trigger.

'You always treat callers this way?' said Herne, watching the small, concentrated eyes behind the gun.

'There's a law in this town against breaking into people's property.'

'I didn't break in, I walked through the door like everyone else.'

'But you intended to go through that door . . . '

72

'Sure I did.'

'And it would have been my duty to have stopped you. That door is private.'

Herne shook his head wonderingly. 'You'd have used that thing?'

'Of course,' she nodded primly.

'Take them duties of yours seriously, don't you?'

'Mister Bellour expects things to be taken care of in his absence.'

'I'll bet he does. Where is he anyway?'

'Mister Bellour is out of town.'

'That's awful convenient.'

'If you came back tomorrow . . .'

'He'll be here tomorrow?'

She almost smiled. 'I don't think so.'

'Then there wouldn't be a lot of point, would there?'

She looked at him, the gun still in her hand, her hand resting on the edge of her polished desk. Somehow her back was still straight like a vice.

'You wouldn't care to tell me where Bellour is so's I could find him?'

The lips pursed and the head moved from side to side like the pendulum of a slow-moving clock.

'You goin' to keep that gun in your hand all day. Liable to scare off custom.'

'The gun stays as long as you do.'

Herne shrugged and gave one final look beyond her to the door. Whatever had been going on back there was doubtless over and done with by now, but if it was nothing more than straight-forward delivery of orders, he couldn't see that it took a gun to keep him away.

He turned on his heels and pushed open the door; for a moment he paused, thinking there might be some final comment, but there was nothing. The door closed to a small ringing of the bell attached above it and when he looked back through the window the gun was out of sight.

Around at the back the delivery wagon had gone and the rear door was locked and bolted, both things as he'd expected. He was turning back into Portsmouth Square when he noticed a carriage coming down the sloping street and pulling to a halt between Bellour's store and the bakers. He didn't recognise the yellow dress or the pale green hat but the turn of the head as the woman got down from the coach assured him that it was Cassie.

She wasn't going to buy sweet rolls.

Herne saw that the carriage was going to wait for her, so he waited too, walking slowly close to the railings inside the park. When he was near enough opposite the store, he saw Cassie's yellow dress before the desk, a glimpse of the woman seated behind it. Cassie seemed to be doing a lot of arm waving and gesticulating and he wondered if things were going to get serious enough again for the woman to get her lethal little toy out from the drawer.

But Cassie turned with a toss of the head and even from that distance, Herne could read the fury on her face.

The door slammed and the bell jangled and she stomped her little feet to the carriage, called up to the driver and climbed in.

Herne set his hands on the railings, climbed swiftly over, dropped to his feet and caught up with the carriage in a few strides. He pulled open the door nearest to him and jumped in.

Cassie gave a sharp little scream, flailed out with her hands and only recognised Herne after he'd seized her and held her arms fast.

She leaned back against the upholstery and he let her go; her tongue, small and pointed, appeared between her lips and she rubbed at her wrists where he'd grabbed them.

'If you'd wanted a ride you could have asked some other way.'

'I wanted to talk.'

'To me?'

'Sure.'

'That's nice.' The teeth did their thing with her lower lip again and she moved a few inches across the space between them; a few inches was all it needed.

'What did you want to talk about?'

'Bellour.'

'I don't know what you mean.'

'Don't play games with me, Cassie.'

Her leg pressed against him and her eyes made it clear that was exactly what she would have liked to do. He watched her eyes as her hand came to rest on his forearm.

'You don't like games?'

'Sometimes.'

'Not now?' she pouted, her fingers tensing in and out on his arm like a cat.

'Right now I want to find out about Bellour.'

'I don't know any Bellour!' she said angrily, tossing her head.

'You just went into his store.'

'Is that his? This Bellour you keep going on about. Bellour. Bellour. Bellour.'

'You didn't want to see him yourself?'

'Of course not.'

'You were looking pretty angry in there. Almost as angry as you look now.'

'I bought a painting there. A week ago. They were supposed to deliver it and it hasn't arrived. Of course I was angry.'

'Just that, huh? A painting that wasn't delivered?'

'That's right.'

'And you don't know Bellour?'

'No, I've told you. No!'

Herne removed her hand and set it back in her lap. 'What do you do when you're not lying, Cassie? If you know when that is, which I doubt.'

She aimed a blow at his face and he deflected her arm high above her head and laughed. 'You'd best keep that temper of yours for something that deserves it. You go on wastin' all your energy like that, you'll be wore out before you come of age.'

He pushed down the handle on the carriage door and jumped out onto the street.

Lucas wasn't any more hospitable than on the previous occasions. He glowered at Herne and asked him what he wanted, seeming annoyed to have to answer that the major was well enough to receive callers.

He led him, not to the billiard room, but the library beyond it. Leather-bound books lined three walls and the fourth held a portrait of the major in dress uniform, sabre drawn.

Major Russell rolled his wheelchair painfully forward, a blanket covering his knees, the swelling around his knuckles larger and darker than before. His face looked drained, the cheeks suddenly sunken in and little more than a flicker of life about the eyes. He looked at the whisky and made a sign that Herne understood meant he should help himself.

'One for you, major?'

'Not now, damn it! Wretched doctor reckons it does something to this heart of mine it shouldn't, though anything that as much as makes it beat I should have thought a good thing.'

'You've been bad?'

'Bad!' Russell snorted. 'I shall soon be a barely breathing corpse rotting to death in this contraption as I roll around this room looking at books I haven't the energy or the patience to read any longer.'

He shook his head and the effort of that alone made him cough and forced him to wipe a line of dark spittle away from his mouth with his sleeve.

'D'you know, Mister Herne, every night of the war I read for half an hour, novels, poetry, getting some kind of peace for myself that blocked out the moaning and crying of the wounded and dying. Now I'm dying myself and I can't find peace inside a book or a bottle of good Scotch whisky.'

His hand lashed out and struck one of the empty glasses from the small table, smashing it against the wall. His head hung down and his eyes closed.

Herne stood his ground, waited.

Several moments later the old man's head came up and the incident was forgotten.

'You've news for me then?'

'Some. I got to see Daniels and told him what you thought about his bits of paper.'

'It doesn't seem from the state of your head to have been a painless encounter – or was that something else?'

'No, that was Daniels all right. Him and the couple of men he keeps with him. But I tore up the i.o.u.s and threw them back in his face. Told him there wasn't any way he's going to collect.'

'You think he believed that?' asked the major sceptically.

'I think he believes I mean it now. I also don't think he liked being talked to that way in front of his bodyguards. My guess is that he'll make one more try to get his money and get his own back on me at the same time.'

'You don't know how?'

'Not yet. It's a matter of keeping my eyes open and waiting to see what breaks.'

'My daughter says someone took a shot at you when you were out riding.'

'Yeah. That looked like Daniels' work, but I don't think it was. I tracked down the fellers who tried to bushwack me and found out who'd paid them to do their dirty work. Seems it was a feller named Bellour – that mean anything to you?'

'Bellour? No, can't say it does. Why should he be interested in you?'

'Right now I don't have the least idea. But I'm working on finding out. One thing I do know, he seems to have some connection with your daughter.'

'Veronica?'

'No.'

'Cassie.' The major's mouth turned down. 'If I wasn't already dying, I swear that child would be the death of me.'

Without knowing exactly why, Herne said: 'How did she get on with Connors?'

The major looked startled, his knotted hands pushing down against the wheels of his chair. 'Why d'you ask that now? What's that got to do with this present affair?'

'I don't know. Nothing maybe.'

'Connors is dead. It's over. There's nothing to be gained from going into it now.'

'Then you don't want me to find out who killed him?'

'Killed him – of course I don't. I never said a thing about it.'

'No, you didn't. But just about everyone else seems to think that's what you brought me here to do.'

He tasted the whisky and wondered if that was what Bellour had thought – and whether that had been reason enough for him to pay to have him killed.

He finished his whisky and set the glass down.

'I'll be going, major. You're tired and I've told you all there is to know. Like I said, I'll wait and see what Daniels is going to pull – and maybe try to find out why this Bellour reckoned it was worth a couple of hundred dollars to see me dead.'

The old man nodded and began to raise his hand in farewell.

Herne turned away fast, eager to be out of the room with a smell of old books and slow dying.

Lucas was waiting in the hallway, right where Herne had expected to find him. He glared out from under his bald head and made it clear that if he ever got the opportunity there wouldn't be anything he'd rather do than break Herne in two.

'Miss Veronica . . . '

'What about her?'

'She's in the parlour. She wants to see you before you go.' His expression made it clear he thought it a serious lapse of taste on Veronica's part, but Herne figured she'd had those before.

She was half-sitting, half-lying on a chaise-longue which was covered in marmalade flowers. She was wearing a white silk dress that clung where it touched and didn't touch most of her very long legs at all. Her hair was down and shone in the light from the fire.

Herne wondered how long it had taken her to perfect her pose, how many rehearsals, how many men had been invited into her parlour to find her in just such a dress, just such a position. He remembered the taste of her mouth and the pressure of her agile tongue, the shape of her breast against his chest.

He looked at the dress falling open on either side of her legs: 'Aren't you afraid of catching cold?'

'I didn't think you were a prude, Jedediah. Although I guess all you cowboys are prudes at heart.' She let a smile play on her face and laughed at him with her eyes. 'You think all us city types are bathed in hell and damnation, don't you?'

'Way I see it, some of you get a mite too close to the fire for comfort.'

'But by the fire's where it's warm, Jedediah?' She patted the space in front of her legs. 'Won't you come and sit over here?'

'I've already been shot at ridin' with you, that's enough danger for one day.'

'The men that did it – did you find out who they were?'

'I caught up with 'em.'

'And did you . . . ?'

'They won't be drygulchin' anyone no more.'

'You killed them?'

'What did you expect me to do? Slap 'em some and tell 'em not to do it again? Besides, they wasn't about to give me a lot of choice.'

'And do you know why they . . . ?'

'Not yet, but I will.'

Veronica lifted the skirt of her dress back over one leg and tucked the other one closer to her body. 'I just bet you will, cowboy.'

'You know a feller name of Bellour?'

She wrinkled her nose a shade as she thought; Herne thought it was the first thing he'd seen her do that suggested she might once have been a little girl.

'I've heard of him. He takes pictures, paints portraits. Very expensive.'

'But you don't *know* him?'

'I don't think so.'

'And Cassie . . . you ever hear her mention him?'

She thought for a minute before shaking her head; a strand of hair caught against her cheek and she freed it with her hand.

'Is it important?'

'I don't know yet.'

'I thought . . .'

'Yeah?'

'I thought you might come to dinner with me tonight.'

'So you can show off your tame cowboy to all your well-to-do friends – no, thanks. I've got as close as I want to to the people you mix with, Daniels and his crowd, and it's only the fact that I took your father's money and made him a promise that keeps me around here any longer.'

Her mouth opened and when the lips came back together they never quite touched. She stood up and the dress shimmered down about her like silver leaves trembled by some passing wind.

'Nothing else to keep you around,' she said softly, disbelievingly. 'Is that the truth, Jedediah?'

Her hand grazed his arm and the tips of her fingers brushed his cheek. He could smell that damn perfume again and the warmth of her body, too. Her eyes had a way of holding his gaze and not easily letting it go.

'There's men who'd do a lot to stay around me, Jedediah. Don't you know that? Don't you know what you have here?'

She smiled and tightened her grip on his shoulder, his neck. She was tall enough to press her mouth to his without straining. Herne let her kiss him, kissed her back. He touched her back and was surprised at the knots of bone that stood so clearly through the flesh; his hand slid over the curve of her behind.

She set her face against his. 'I'm sorry about earlier.'

'That's okay.'

'Good.' Her skin was soft as the silk of her dress, softer. 'The dining room at the Palace Hotel . . .'

'Uh-uh.' He disentangled her arms, stepped back. 'I told you, I've got things to do. A job to finish. When your father paid me, it wasn't to escort you to dinner . . . or anywhere else.'

Veronica's face froze cold and expressionless: she moved

back to the chaise longue and lit a cigarette. Smoke curled from the edges of her mouth as Herne closed the door on her and walked under Lucas's disapproving stare to the front door.

Chapter Eight

The night was warm and the clouds slipped across the moon like they had places to go and little enough time to keep. The stars seemed to burn out of the velvet black. Herne had been watching the gang of kids congregating in the corner of the park, thirty of them by now, talking loudly, the occasional small fight breaking out between them to be cheered on and finally broken up. They had a small fire going and Herne could see the occasional flicker of a blade in its orange light, but mostly they seemed to be armed with pick handles and clubs, one or two carrying iron railings they'd yanked clear from the broken sections of the park fence.

A couple of policemen appeared at the far side of the park, walked some way towards them before turning off by the liberty pole and minding their own business.

A light burned in back of Bellour's store and Herne stuck to the shadows and waited.

A black cat with one ear and a high-arching back came and rubbed itself against his boot but Herne was unimpressed. After a few minutes the cat lost interest; inside the store the light stayed on. Three or four of the punk kids from the gang were wandering up and down the street outside the mail company office, banging their sticks on the railings and hollering at the tops of their voices.

The smooth wood of the Colt's butt was reassuring against Herne's hand.

The light went out.

Herne's breath clogged in his throat.

The back door opened cautiously and he eased himself deeper back into the shadows.

There wasn't enough light to see the man's face clearly,

but Herne guessed that it was the same one he'd briefly seen earlier, poking round the door while he'd been speaking to the receptionist with the handy little gun and the winning smile.

He waited to see which direction the man was heading after he'd locked the door. Carefully, he slid in behind him and followed some fifty yards behind on the opposite side of the street. There were quite a few people about now so he didn't stick out. In any case, the man gave no indication that he thought he might be being followed.

If Herne had been hoping the feller would have led him directly to Bellour he was mistaken. He went into a bar called the *Pleasant Valley* and sat down at a booth midway along. Herne could see the sandy hair clearly now, the open face and the cracked tooth as he asked the waitress for a beer.

He hoped it wasn't going to be a long wait.

Three beers later, he wasn't so sure. The man didn't look like he was anxious to shift before either the bar closed or he was too drunk to ask for another. He was drinking with the determination of a man with something on his mind he was doing his best to rub out. Herne knew that if he waited too long, he wouldn't get the information out of him he wanted – and that would only mean hanging around in San Francisco longer than he wished.

He was figuring the best way to get inside and force the feller out when to his surprise, the man shook his head at the waitress, lurched to his feet, pulled some money from his pocket and dropped it down onto her tray and headed for the door.

He walked faster now, like he'd made up his mind about something. The streets were narrower and there were less people about and Herne had trouble not being spotted.

After ten minutes, the man turned into a three-storey building with a sign out front that advertised rooms by the week, the night or the hour.

The lobby had a length of carpet whose pattern had long ago got lost in the scrapings of filthy boots and the scars of cigar butts. A smeared spitoon rested against the side of a worn-out settee, tired from overuse. Back of a small counter, a thin man whose head had bust through the straggle of his hair was pretending to read a newspaper.

Herne glanced at the stairs, set one hand on the counter and asked which room the man who'd just come in had gone to.

'I don't know what . . . '

Herne ripped the paper from his hands and grabbed hold of the clerk's greasy shirt front. He'd spent enough time waiting around and he was getting impatient.

The clerk should have understood this but he didn't.

He tried stalling Herne some more.

Herne shifted hands on the shirt and showed the clerk the barrel of his Colt from close quarters.

'Nineteen. Third floor.' The clerk spluttered and tried not to look at the gun which was pressed against the bridge of his nose.

'If you're lyin' . . . '

'I ain't lyin'. Honest, I ain't.'

Herne pushed him back down into his chair and the chair skidded the short distance against the wall.

By that time Herne was half way up the first flight of stairs. The higher he got the less light there was and the richer and more varied the smells grew. The carpet petered out after the first landing.

Nineteen had the one missing but it was the room he was looking for. A lamp glowed dully at the end of the corridor and voices came from behind the door, a man and a woman. Herne wondered if the door was locked and what would happen if he charged in. He thought there was only one way to find out – if the handle didn't do his work for him.

It gave to his touch.

Three quarters slow and quiet and then the last part fast, leaning his weight against the door and bringing up his Colt as he pushed forward.

There was a bed with the covers pulled across midway, a table with a few glasses and a bottle of whisky, a sagging armchair and a couple of straightbacked chairs with burn marks liberally scattered over them, a scarred dresser and not a lot else. The window at the back was part open and the breeze was just managing to shift the cotton material that hung down across it.

The sandy-haired man was half in, half out of the armchair, his hand reaching towards what might have been a gun in his coat pocket.

The woman from the store was standing close by the window. Her mouth opened to a red gash and stared at Herne, at the gun in his hand. Her hair was still tight and precise, her clothes as perfectly arranged, the red on her fingernails was still as vivid and dark.

'What the hell . . . ?' began the man.

'Shut it!' snapped Herne and moved the gun round to cover him.

'You can't come bustin' in here . . . '

'Jerry, he just did,' said the woman with evident scorn.

'That's right, Jerry,' said Herne, and kicked back with his boot, slamming the door shut. 'Now move your hand real slow and lift out whatever you got stashed in that pocket of yours and set it down on the table real careful.'

The eyes flickered hesitantly and the mouth formed words that never got spoken.

'Do it!' Herne said.

The woman laughed, a short, bitter sound.

Jerry removed a pistol from his pocket and laid it on the table.

'He can't use it anyway,' the woman said sarcastically.

'I'm surprised to find you in a place like this,' said Herne, glancing round.

'Not as surprised as I am myself. Except I have this habit of picking born losers who think they're goin' to be winners but never as much as get into the race.'

'Shut up!' called Jerry, flushed.

'Shut up yourself!' she snapped back with such force, he collapsed back into the sagging chair and looked like a six year old kid whose sarsaparilla had just been taken from him.

'What do you want?' the woman asked.

'Same as before. I want to see Bellour.'

'That all?'

'Maybe.'

'Evelyn, don't . . . ' Jerry tried.

'I told you to shut up and leave this to me. You already led him here, isn't that enough for one night?'

He scowled, but not so as she could see him. Herne wondered if she ever drove him so far he hit back, but doubted it.

Evelyn came a few paces away from the window towards him and Herne realised she wasn't unlike Veronica Russell — a shade shorter, perhaps, a slightly fuller figure, her face not quite as oval, but they seemed to have been cut from similar moulds. Maybe it was something living in San Francisco did to a woman. Maybe Cassie would get to look like that if she ever got out of playing at being an eight year old with a cute way of biting her lower lip.

'If we tell you you'll leave us alone?'

'Sure.'

'And you won't tell Bellour how you found out where he was.'

'Uh-uh.'

'All right. He's got a place on Union Street, near Telegraph Hill. It's a narrow wooden building painted white and black. You can't miss it, it's just above the intersection with Kearney.'

'He'll be there now?'

'Now or later.'

'And if he isn't there?'

'He'll be gambling somewhere, that's what he usually . . . '

'Cord Daniel's place?'

Her eyes narrowed keenly. 'How did you know that?'

'I didn't. I guessed.'

She and Jerry exchanged glances that Herne couldn't read.

'One more thing,' he began.

'You said that was all.'

'Never mind that. The girl who came in after me . . . '

'What about her?'

'What did she want?'

'The same as you.'

'Bellour.'

'That's right.'

'What did you tell her?'

'The same thing. He wasn't there.'

'Did you tell her where she could find him?'

Evelyn moved her head to one side and laughed.

'What's so funny?' asked Herne.

'That little bitch has known where to find Bellour for long enough, that's what's funny.'

'What's between them?'

She laughed again, the same brittle, bitter sound. 'Not a lot, you can be sure of that.'

'I don't understand,' said Herne.

She looked at him pityingly. 'No, you don't look as if you would. Strong, mainly silent type. Sleeps with his horse and keeps his little woman back on some ranch somewhere, getting up before dawn to milk cows but always waiting in her gingham apron around sundown, an apple pie warming on the stove, her silly little face turned towards the horizon just in case he rides out of the golden glow.'

'Shut your mouth!' shouted Herne, taking a stride towards her, wanting nothing as much as to drive the barrel of his Colt hard across her mocking face.

His stride took him past the table and for a second he lost sight of what the man was doing.

Jerry jumped quicker than Herne would have given him credit for and grabbed the gun. Herne turned a moment later and swung down with his right hand. Jerry's finger jerked awkwardly against the trigger and the bullet went wide of Herne, wide of the woman and tore at the curtain, shattering the pane of glass and sending splinters down into the street below.

The underside of the Colt came down hard on Jerry's arm and he yelled and let go the gun.

Herne stepped in fast and kicked it over towards the door. He lifted the Colt clear and punched Jerry's jaw with his left hand.

The blow sent him over onto his back, then groaning

onto his side, curled up alongside the bed.

Evelyn snorted in disgust and stared down at him like she was staring at all the other lost opportunities and broken promises her life had been made up of.

Herne ignored Jerry and spoke to her. 'What's goin' on with you an' him an' Bellour? You doin' some double-dealin' behind his back or what?'

She snorted again. 'That was another of his big ideas. A quick way to make money.' She gestured round the room. 'Look at this. I was fool enough to believe him. A feller who lives in a stinkin' dump like this an' he talks about making money the easy way!'

'How were you going to make this money from Bellour. Just by holding back what he got for his paintings or what?'

She laughed and shook her head. On the floor, Jerry was slowly sitting up, rubbing gingerly at his chin. 'You got a lot to learn, mister.'

There were shouts coming up from the street below and footsteps loud on the stairs outside. Herne glanced round at the door, back at Evelyn and made his move. When the door sprang open and an arm came in with a gun at the end of it, he chopped down hard and the gun fell towards the floor. Herne grasped the arm and yanked it into the room. A startled face came towards him and he sank the butt of the Colt into the middle of it and it disappeared from sight. There were two more men bulking outside the door, brandishing weapons. Herne didn't know who they were and he didn't have time to ask. There were questions he wanted to ask Evelyn, but there wasn't time for those either. It was Bellour who held the answers and he wanted to get there fast. He swung the Colt round towards the landing and the two men backed off and dropped their guns to the floor, kicking them away when Herne told them.

He had one more look round at Evelyn, looking sore as Hell over by the window, her loser sitting with his head in his hands nursing his jaw and what was left of his pride.

Herne took the stairs three at a time and when he listened for the sound of men following him there was nothing.

Chapter Nine

The house was painted black on the ground floor, white above. A rounded bay window was covered with white shutters through which narrow lines of light filtered out onto the street. The sounds of a piano trickled out with them. Herne ignored the front door in favour of the rear. When it proved to be locked he drew the bayonet from his boot and forced the door open.

There were no lights on the ground floor and the music was coming from above.

He found the stairs and climbed them quiet as he could.

The piano melody was tinkling, not quite in key, a sound like a child who hadn't perfected the technique for the piece that was being played.

The door to the room at the front of the house was closed, a filter of light showing through onto the dark carpet. Herne freed the hammer of the Colt and tried the door handle.

The wood swished back, barely touching the covered floor.

Immediately Herne was aware of a sickly-sweet smell that he guessed to be opium. The air inside the room was close and warm, but he pushed the door shut rather than risk being disturbed. He moved to the window and lifted the lower section, while leaving the shutters fastened.

The room was lit by a lamp the shade of which had been painted red and a dull and dark glow shone over everything, leaving the corners lost in misty shadow.

Most things in the room were white. A bear rug was spread across the centre of the floor and to one side of it there was a leather settee in white hide. Tables, chairs and sideboards were also white. On the opposite side of the room to the settee was a grand piano, but this was black, a glass vase standing before the raised lid and holding white lilies.

There was an opium pipe set up on the small table alongside the empty fireplace.

Cassie continued to play the piano.

She was wearing a white bridal veil, held around her head by a twined circle of white and red flowers. White lace fingerless gloves rose to just below her elbows. Small white satin shoes on her feet.

She was oblivious to Herne's presence and other than the veil, the gloves and the shoes she was quite naked.

Her fingers moved awkwardly across the keys and she stared down at them, as if concentrating, trying to remember.

'Cassie.'

Herne's voice was hollow in the sweetness of the room, hollow and out of place.

'Cassie!'

She gave no sign of having heard him and Herne was certain that she hadn't. He didn't think she could hear anything other than the melody she was playing and maybe something that was going on deep inside her head.

Even with the air that was entering the room from the freshly-opened window, Herne found that the opium was making his head swim. He knew that Cassie wasn't about to go anywhere of her own accord. He went out of the room and began to search the house. The first room along the corridor was a bedroom, the large four-poster bed covered in black satin. A riding whip hung from the post to the right of the satin pillows.

The scent in the room was more subtle, feminine.

The only clothes in sight were male.

He tried the next room and found the door locked. The bayonet soon gained him access. He struck a match against the butt of the Colt and lit a lamp that was standing on the table at the far side of the room.

Bellour's camera was set up in the centre of the room and immediately in front of it was a small bed covered in a white silk sheet. The sheet was crumpled and smeared with small stains. In a wardrobe in the corner hung a number of items of female clothing, including small girls' dresses. On the floor between the wardrobe and the bed lay a thick leather belt and a silk handkerchief with lace at the edges. The silk was dark with something that might have been dried blood.

The exhibits which hung on the walls were different from those which Bellour kept on display in his store.

Girls wearing a few selected items of clothing; girls wearing nothing but a pouting smile and a look of assumed innocence; girls who cuddled teddy bears or licked large lollypops or oversize dummies; girls who cuddled whips to their small breasts with a gaze of aging innocence; girls who lifted or stretched or spread their legs for Bellour's camera; girls who kissed the air in front of it, laughed at it, winked at it, pointed at it as if to say, 'I know what you're peeking at!'

Not all of the girls were Cassie, but most of them looked like her. It was Cassie, though, who held pride of place. Cassie whose poses were the most daring, the most debauched, Herne guessed the most in demand from discerning collectors.

He didn't know how large a trade there was in such items there in San Francisco, but he guessed that it would be big, pretty big. He guessed that a great deal of money would change hands. He wondered how much, if any, found its way into Cassie's hands.

He was opening and closing drawers, leafing through piles and piles of pictures and looking for something which might provide him with more concrete information when he became aware that the piano playing had stopped.

He straightened, hand to his gun uncertain if the sound had ceased that second or if he had only slowly become aware of the silence.

Carefully, he went out into the corridor.

There was a light down below.

He followed it into what proved to be large sitting room with expensive and comfortable furniture and a selection of Bellour's more respectable work on the walls.

Cassie was still dressed as a bride – if dressed was an

adequate word — and she was holding a lamp high in her right hand. She was staring down at the carpet between the tiled fireplace and the low, circular table.

Herne, his stomach sickened already by what he had found upstairs, followed her gaze.

The body of a man he presumed to be Ray Bellour was stretched out flat, legs spread wide, one arm reaching towards the fire, the other high over his head. For some time he had been bleeding onto what was without doubt a very fine and expensive Indian patterned carpet. Most of the blood had begun to dry and it clung to the pile in ridges like miniature waves. The wound from which the blood had flowed was sagging open at his neck, like some grotesque version of Evelyn's red mouth.

Herne knelt close.

Whatever had been used had been thick and jagged, not a knife but the edge of a broken bottle or something similar. The head had been forced back and the skin slashed through several times until there was an ugly wound that spread almost from ear to ear.

Herne's stomach clenched tight and for a moment he thought the combination of the opium and the pictures and now this slaughtered body might make him vomit.

He stood up and turned towards Cassie.

She was looking at him intently, as if aware now for the first time that he was there. The hand holding the lamp was folding over and those teeth were beginning to slot into the constant impressions they had already made in her lower lip.

He caught the lamp just in time and set it on the mantelpiece, where it flickered for a moment, threatened to gutter and go out, but finally held and cast strong shadows across the room.

Cassie started to laugh, a high-pitched distant giggling that ran Herne's nerves raw.

He slapped her face once and the giggling subsided, slapped her again and it stopped and she was suddenly conscious of what was going on around her. She stared past Herne at the body on the carpet, clutched one hand to her mouth and vomited over one of the armchairs before she could turn further away.

Herne watched her pathetic body as it folded across the chair, vomit trailing from her fingers and the corners of her open mouth.

He found a cloth and helped her to wipe herself dry. She looked at him and shivered against him, but he pushed her away and told her to go and find her clothes. For a moment it didn't seem as though she had understood him, but something in her expression suggested that perhaps she did, so Herne left her and went back to the room above.

For ten minutes he found every picture of Cassie that he could, dumped them into a box and carried them back down.

Cassie was half dressed, the absurd wedding veil still attached to her head. Angry, Herne snatched it away and ordered her to hurry. He tipped the pictures into the open hearth and set fire to them with matches, leaning over them as they caught and shrivelled, their brown tints darkening and darkening as their sickening images gradually disappeared from sight. One after another they curled and twisted while the body of their maker lay a few feet away, eyes closed and throat open, seeing nothing.

Cassie stood before him, dressed, shivering.

She looked, for the first time, genuinely young – not a pretence or a game, a show that she'd found pleased others and into which she'd got trapped, but a frightened young girl who was gradually coming to realise what had taken place.

Herne put his hand on her shoulder and moved her towards the door and the street.

Lucas opened the door and as soon as he saw the apparent state Cassie was in, his lip curled back over his teeth and he bellowed out a roar of rage. His fist swung back and came for Herne's head like a hammer. Herne swayed inside it just, the thumb catching his ear. He tried to throw a punch of his own, but the black had him against the door frame and was not giving him any room. They struggled for several moments, each one trying to get a clear blow at the other without success.

Finally, Lucas pulled back to aim a blow to Herne's face and gave Herne the opportunity to drive his elbow hard into the black's ribs. It didn't shift him backwards, but at least it stopped him in his tracks. Herne quickly threw a left to his head and tried to bury his right fist in his solar plexus; Lucas responded by taking two steps back, bellowing louder than before and charging Herne with his head down.

Herne tried to side step but the charge didn't leave him much time. The bald skull struck the top of his shoulder and cannoned off, knocking Herne back into the doorway just as Veronica was walking through it. He grabbed at the sides of the frame to keep himself from falling over or colliding with her and while his arms were outstretched, Lucas charged again.

Herne caught at Lucas's neck as the head drove deep into his belly and the two of them went rolling back onto the drive and towards the shrubs.

Herne managed to kick out his right leg and catch Lucas a glancing blow on the knee, halting him from rising for a few seconds. Time enough for Herne to swing a fist into the side of his jaw and follow up with another between the eyes.

Lucas's head went back and his eyes closed as if Herne had actually managed to hurt him.

He wasn't taking any chances.

He stepped back, swung his right leg, and planted the underside of his boot alongside the black's temple.

Lucas went down poleaxed and didn't show any immediate signs of getting up.

From the safety of the doorway, Veronica Russell clapped her gloved hands together in mock applause. Then she turned away, stepped into the house and saw Cassie.

'My God! What . . . ?'

'Never mind now. Is there someone who can put her to bed? Sit with her? I don't want her going back out and I don't want anyone to know she's here. When Lucas comes round tell him not to let anyone into the house and to say that Cassie's been here all along.'

'What's happened?'

'Never mind for now. Can you do what I said?'

'Of course. But . . . '

'All right. I'm going to wash up if you'll show me where. After you've handled things we can talk.'

Veronica wasn't used to taking orders but she sensed that in this case it was the right thing to do. She pointed Herne in the direction he wanted and got on with what she had to do.

She brought him a large glass of whiskey and a cup of strong coffee. Herne didn't know what time it was but guessed it had to be very late. He hoped the major was sleeping and that he wouldn't have to be told the half of what had happened – if Herne himself ever got to know that much.

Veronica had found time to change into a straightforward blouse and a calf-length skirt and she looked about as ordinary as Herne supposed she ever got – which was not very.

He drank half the whiskey, a couple of mouthfuls of coffee and told her what he knew.

She stood listening, her face lengthening, eyes darkening at every sentence. When Herne had finished she took the glass from his hand and downed the rest of the whisky in a swallow.

'You think Cassie killed him?' she said, her voice controlled and matter-of-fact.

Herne shrugged: 'I think she could have. When you've been on that stuff you can do most anything and not know a damn thing about it.'

'Half Chinatown spends its time in opium dens – they don't seem to do too bad on it.'

'Maybe they're more used to it than Cassie.'

'Sure. And maybe not. I knew she'd been running pretty wild, but . . . '

'Didn't you try and do something about it?'

'Oh, sure,' she gestured, beginning to pace the room. 'I'd talk with her and get my words spat back in my face. Once in a while I'd even talk with dad but it only ate into his

bones a little more. What was he supposed to do? Besides —
she's a grown girl now. But you've seen those pictures. You
know that for yourself.'

Herne turned his head away. He found it hard to
understand that two girls could be so uncaring of one
another when they shared the same blood—except that
maybe that was at the root of it. The same wild blood. No
wonder the old man was rotting in his bed or that damned
wheel chair of his, decay seeping into him from every part
of his body.

'Did you know about them?'

'Cassie's artistic poses? No, but it doesn't surprise me.'

'Doesn't it sicken you?'

She looked at him, hesitating. 'It upsets me, sure. It
upsets me to think that someone like Bellour has been
making a small fortune out of my sister's body. But if
anything sickens me it's the minds of the men who need to
buy that stuff. It's them who're sick, not Cassie. If she gets
corrupted by it, it's their corruption she's contaminated by.'

She spun away and seized a vase from one of the small
rosewood tables and hurled it against the opposite wall.
The thin glass shattered and splinters sprayed out into the
room like sharp rain.

'You're all the same! Daniels. Bellour. You. Every man I
ever met!'

Herne shook his head. There were things he could say to
try and prove that she was wrong but words wouldn't make
a dent in what her life had shown her. He finished his coffee
and waited for her to calm down, the fine lines of her face
slowly relaxing, her body becoming less tense.

'I'm sorry. Maybe you didn't deserve that. Not after
what you did getting Cassie out of there.'

'It's okay.'

She came over and sat opposite him, her eyes were wide
and dark and tired and he thought there were traces of
vulnerability about her for the first time but even then he
couldn't be sure.

'What can we do about Cassie?'

Herne looked at her, looked at the floor, back at

Veronica again. 'In the long term, I don't know. Maybe you can get her a doctor, straighten her out, send her away. I don't know. But now, keep her in and out of sight. So far as I can see there's no one who can link her with what happened to Bellour. If . . . '

Her fingers grazed his forearm. 'Are you saying you don't care if she's guilty?'

'What's guilty? What does that mean after what he's done to her? For what it's worth I don't think she cut his throat, but I wouldn't blame her if she did. I'll poke around, ask a few questions. If I can find out who did do it, then she's off the hook for good.'

Her hand closed round his wrist. 'Thanks, cowboy.'

Herne stood up and she released her grip. 'Don't thank me yet.'

At the door he turned. 'Would Lucas have gone wild like that if that'd been you I'd brought back in that state?'

'Lucas has always been specially fond of Cassie. Her and my father both. There's something special about them as far as he's concerned.'

'An' he'd do anything to protect them?'

She looked at him sharply. 'If he could, yes. Why d'you . . . ?'

But the door had closed on Herne's back and Veronica's question went unasked.

Chapter Ten

Herne asked for his steak well done and with a couple of eggs on the top, a side order of fried potatoes and some tomatoes. While he was waiting for it to arrive he drank black coffee from a tall, thick china mug and thought over what he knew.

What he thought he knew.

There was one man who might have good reason to want him dead and that was Cord Daniels, but the one who'd put a price on his head had been Ray Bellour. At the time Bellour hadn't any reason for knowing him at all. Except that Cassie knew about him and had made her own guesses about what he was doing. And Cassie could have told Bellour. But Cassie, like everyone else, thought the major had hired him to find out what had happened just before Connors was dragged out of the bay with his throat cut.

Which was precisely what had happened to Bellour himself.

If Bellour had wanted to keep Herne from finding out about Connors it meant one of two things: either Connors had found out about the racket in dirty pictures and Bellour didn't want Herne coming down the same trail, or Bellour had been responsible for having Connors killed and wanted to head Herne off from tracking that one home.

One of two things – or both.

The second as a consequence of the first.

He leaned back as the waitress set down a large oval plate, a second plate for his tomatoes and potatoes, a third holding two thick wedges of cornbread.

'More coffee?' She was freckle-faced, auburn haired, her arms were tanned and slightly fat; when she smiled a dimple appeared smack in the centre of her left cheek. Herne thought she looked just about the only natural woman he'd seen since he'd got to San Francisco.

'Sure,' he said, smiling back. 'It's good.'

The smile didn't last long.

He'd remembered one other connection, one other way. When he'd suggested to Evelyn that Bellour could have been gambling at Daniels' place, the idea had struck home hard. If there was a connection between the two men that was more than co-incidental; if Daniels was in some way wrapped up in Bellour's dirty racket; if he knew about Cassie . . .

Herne leaned back and let the idea run through his mind a little more. He could see it all beginning to draw together . . . maybe . . . just maybe.

'Is something wrong?' He realised that the waitress was standing beside him, concern on her face.

'No, why d'you ask?'

'You've hardly touched your breakfast.'

He glanced down at the steak and shook his head, gave a short laugh. 'It's fine. I was thinking, that's all.'

'You shouldn't make a habit of it.'

'Thinking? I don't.'

She grinned. 'Enjoy your steak now.'

He nodded, smiled, watched her as she walked away towards one of the other tables. Then he turned his attentions back to his meal, eating now with even greater appetite, excited by the fact that he could feel himself about to break through the maze at last.

He listened to the newsboy's shout of 'Painter found dead in Bay!' and bought a paper. According to the front page story the body of Raymond Bellour, noted society portrait painter and artist, had been discovered floating in the bay by fishermen returning at first light. His throat had been cut and his wallet was missing. San Francisco police were working on the assumption that the murder was yet another carried out by the gangs of wild youths which continued to terrorise sections of the city after dark.

Herne folded the newspaper and tapped it against his thigh. Someone had gone into the house after he and Cassie had left, removed Bellour's body and dumped it in the bay. Either the killer had come back or someone else had found the dead man and not wanted the death to be thought of as anything other than a violent crime that had taken place out on the streets.

Who might have gone to the Bellour house in his wake?

Who knew that he was going there in the first place?

He tossed the paper back to the astonished boy and hurried off in the direction of Portsmouth Square.

The blinds were still pulled down over the plate glass window at the front of the store and the door was locked, the closed sign still in place. Herne didn't even bother trying the lock.

The rear door was open and he walked through and almost bumped smack into the back of a short, stocky man wearing a plaid overcoat and a bowler hat.

The man shouted and turned and at the same moment a uniformed policeman came through from the front of the store.

Herne apologised and turned away but he wasn't going to get out that easily.

The man under the bowler hat was the police officer in charge of the investigation into Bellour's death. He spoke with the remains of a Scottish accent and his breath smelt equally of bourbon and peppermint. He set himself between Herne and the street and quizzed him closely about what he was doing walking into the back entrance of a place whose owner had just been fished out of the water with his throat slit from one ear to the other.

Herne said that he'd been into the place the previous day to see about getting a picture made that he could take back to his family in Wyoming. The owner hadn't been there and he'd been told to come back the next day, which was what he was doing. The front had been shut so he'd tried the back. He didn't know anything about the owner being killed. He hardly ever read the papers.

To be honest, he shrugged, he had more than a little difficulty with reading.

The policeman looked at him carefully, weighing his words against his appearance and the look of the Colt .45 holstered at his side. He didn't look anyone's fool – not a city man, of course, but not a fool either.

Finally he asked Herne for the address he was using in the city and nodded when he was told the name of the hotel.

'Staying long in San Francisco?'

'Not long now.'

'But I daresay you'll be around for the next day or two?'

Herne nodded, assured him that he would. There was nothing else to add. He walked slowly away, making sure that no one was paying any attention to where he was going.

As soon as he was sure he was in the clear, he set off for the cheap hotel where he'd left Evelyn and Jerry the night before. The night clerk had been replaced by a fat man with the face of a twelve year old boy and an incongruous pipe curling down from the corner of his young mouth.

The clerk eyed Herne up and down and reached around for a key, figuring he'd just got into town and was looking for a bed.

Herne looked at the key and shook his head. 'There's a couple in room nineteen.'

'Not any more there ain't.' The clerk took his pipe from his mouth as he talked, staring down at the bowl now and preparing to poke it with the stem of a burnt-out match.

'Last night . . . '

'Last night there was trouble up there. Guns bein' fired off an' all sorts apparently. Feller up there did serious damage to one of the staff an' threatened to shoot innocent passers-by who'd run in to see what was happening. We couldn't let them stay here after that.'

He succeeded in tamping down his tobacco, struck a fresh match and sucked hard two or three times until he was satisfied it was burning again.

'Friends of yours?'

'Sort of.'

'Funny kind of friends.' He stared at Herne quizzically and Herne wondered how much he'd been told about the appearance of the man who'd been causing all the trouble.

'Know where they've gone?'

'Search me, feller. But you can bet they won't've strayed more'n two or three blocks of here. They ain't got the money for nothin' better an' unless they're goin' to sleep rough down on the docks, there ain't a lot else to choose from. Not in this town.'

Herne nodded, grunted thanks and left him to his pipe.

His feet were sore and his temper short when he found them and then it was as much by luck as anything else. That and Jerry's tendency to poke his head round the wrong door at the wrong time.

Herne had finished asking the woman scrubbing the lobby of the *El Camino Real* about any couple who'd moved in fresh that morning and taken her assurances that they hadn't had a new customer inside the last week never mind the last twenty-four hours, when the entrance door swung back and there was Jerry with a loaf of bread in one hand and a bag of fruit in the other.

He saw Herne and yelped, dropping the fruit and hurling the bread. Herne ducked under it easily and set off after him. Jerry skidded on the stones outside, recovered his balance and tried to sprint for cover.

Herne got to within four feet and dived.

His arms wrapped themselves around Jerry's legs and the two of them crashed to the ground. Herne landed on his shoulder and rolled to the right, pushing himself up with one hand and one foot. Jerry was still kneeling and winded.

Herne grabbed the back of his shirt collar and lifted him to his feet.

Jerry looked hangdog away. 'Evelyn's gonna kill me for this.'

She was waiting in the back room on the first floor. It was even more of a dump than the place they'd been thrown out of and the half dozen of Bellour's portraits looked out of place stacked against the walls. What lay on the bed, scattered this way and that, seemed more at home.

Herne obviously hadn't found Bellour's entire collection of dirty _ictures.

Evelyn was wearing a fawn sweater with puffed-up sleeves and a mouth that was determinedly turned down at the corners. When she saw Jerry walk into the room with Herne close at his back she sighed and shook her head in disgust.

'You can't even get somethin' to eat without . . . '

'He got the food all right,' interrupted Herne, 'he just threw it all over the lobby. You're lucky this isn't another hotel you're being thrown out of.'

Evelyn scowled at him and rubbed her knuckles against her hip. She hadn't bothered to make up her lips and her mouth looked close to normal for the first time since Herne had seen her.

She flopped down in a chair and it came close to giving way under her. 'What have you come for now? To gloat?'

Herne made sure he was where he could see Jerry, in case the sandy-haired feller had another rush of courage to the head. He didn't think it was very likely but he felt he was too close to take unnecessary chances.

'I got some more questions.'

'This time you can pay for the answers.'

'Like Bellour did?'

'What's that supposed to mean?'

'Don't tell me you didn't hear the news?' He pointed to the paintings and pictures. 'I can see you went down to the store before the police got there and took away a few souvenirs of your late boss.'

'He owed us more than that,' she scowled.

'Maybe,' said Herne, moving towards her. 'Enough to kill him with a broken bottle drawn across his throat?'

'What the hell are you talking about?' She was on her feet and leaning towards him, fear and anger mixed together in her face, tight and intense in her eyes.

'We read about it in the paper,' put in Jerry, 'that was all we knew.'

Evelyn clicked her tongue against the roof of her mouth

and looked at him in disgust.

'If you'd waited that long,' said Herne, 'you'd never have got all this stuff out in time. No, you knew where I was going and you followed. Maybe one of you, maybe both. You got there and found no trace of me but there was Bellour's body. Maybe you figured if you left it there the law would start asking too many questions close to home. So you tipped him in the bay and let them think it was a robbery that went a little too far. Less chance you'd get questioned. More chance you could sell this junk.' He glanced round at the bed. 'That filth!'

'It ain't true,' protested Jerry, leaning back against the wall, looking sulky and sorry for himself.

Herne wondered not for the first time what there was about him that had attracted Evelyn to him in the first place – aside from her admitted attraction to losers.

'You'd better hope it's true,' said Herne, ''cause if it ain't there's one other way of dealin' the cards that I can see an' that leaves you with a worse hand than before.'

'What's that, smart-ass?' asked Evelyn sourly.

'You'd already been to see him that night. You fought, argued, he got his throat cut and you left him to bleed to death. You already knew he was there on the carpet when you sent me over.'

'That don't make any sense!' Evelyn screamed back at him, her hands raking the air.

'Maybe not. But I was just talking to a policeman with a bowler hat and a Scottish accent who'd like to try it for size.'

She shook her head and collapsed back in the chair.

'Best tell him what he wants, honey,' began Jerry.

'You shut up!' she yelled and dug her nails into the fraying upholstery at the side of the chair.

She stared at the threadbare rug and the life seemed to fade out of her.

'What d'you want?' she asked Herne, not looking at him, her voice barely audible.

'I want the truth about last night. That'll do for a start.'

'Okay.' She breathed deep and waited. 'Part of it was like

you said. We went along to Bellour's house after you. We'd have gone sooner but there was so many people runnin' round that crummy hotel squawking and carryin' on, we was lucky to get out at all. By the time we got there, you must've left. The back door was open and we got half way in when we heard someone else comin' in the front.'

Herne looked at her with added interest and as if sensing this she drew herself up and looked at him direct, life returning to her voice.

'We laid low and watched what happened. We hadn't been there five minutes when these two fellers came out the back carryin' this body. It was Bellour right enough. They slung him in the back of a wagon an' headed off towards the bay. That was all we saw of 'em. We went in and found half of Bellour's blood on the carpet in front of the fire. A mess of ashes like someone had been trying hard to get rid of something they didn't want anyone to see. First we thought his whole stock had been cleared out, but we found those locked away.' She was looking over at the bed, shaking her head. 'You know how much money you burned up in that grate? You got any idea?'

'I know I'd've burnt that heap there if I'd found 'em.'

'There's thousands of dollars in blackened paper an' ash wasted in that house. Thousands of dollars!'

Herne scooped up a pile of pictures from the bed and held them up towards her. 'Don't it matter to you that you're making money out of this heap of shit?'

'Why should it? If I don't sell it, someone else will. If Bellour hadn't peddled that muck, someone else would have.'

'But you're a woman, God damn it!'

'Sure,' she laughed bitterly. 'Sure an' what are you? Who d'you think it is pays for that stuff? Men like you.'

'Not like me.'

'All men are like you. All men are the same.' She pushed herself up out of the chair and and went to the window and looked down onto the street. 'That's not right,' she said, talking for her own sake as much as anyone else's, 'there's two kinds of men, those with guns in their hands who know how to use 'em and those who don't. I always end up with those who don't.'

She spun round and stared at Herne hard.

'Anything else we can do for you, mister?'

For answer he turned and flicked the pictures one over the other, checking quickly to see if any were of Cassie.

'I thought you weren't interested in that stuff.'

'I'm not.'

'It don't look like it.'

Cassie wasn't there. He felt like putting a match to these as well, but he knew that what the woman had said was right and that if he got rid of them there would be others to take their place.

'You finished with us?' said Evelyn sourly.

Jerry was still leaning against the wall, as though while Herne was in the room he was afraid to as much as move.

'Almost,' Herne replied.

'Get it over with.'

'These two men you say carried out Bellour's body . . .'

'I don't just say, they were there. You think we made 'em up or something?'

'Okay, these two, you recognise 'em?

'I never saw them before.'

'You?' asked Herne, looking at Jerry.

'Never.'

'But you know what they looked like?'

'It was dark,' said Evelyn. 'It was night, remember.'

'Not that dark. You must've seen something.'

She hesitated, plucking at the threads coming loose from the top of the chair. 'What's it worth?'

'Me not talking to the police. Telling them you were there. Where they can find you now.'

'How do we know you ain't goin' to do that anyway?' said Jerry.

'You'll just have to trust me.'

Evelyn snorted and snapped off a thread between her fingers. She didn't like it but she knew they didn't have any choice.

'One of them was big, built like a house. He could have

been Chinese or something.'

'The other small?'

'Sure. A little feller. Half his size. They had trouble balancing Bellour between them. Maybe he was starting to go stiff.'

Herne had heard all he needed to know.

'You know them?' Evelyn asked, but she didn't really expect him to answer.

Herne paused in the doorway. 'Be good to one another.'

When the door closed he heard the wrangling start going down. All the way along the corridor and down the stairs he could smell the sourness of damp bedding and stale air and people forced to feed on one another's weakness. Out front the street didn't seem to offer a whole lot better.

Chapter Eleven

He wasn't in any mood for back doors.

When Quinlan flipped open the spy panel and peered out, the barrel of Herne's Colt poked between the Irishman's eyes.

'You got five seconds to open this door or you're a dead man.'

It took three and a half.

Quinlan stood well back with his hands in the air and an expression of impish glee on his face that Herne failed to understand.

'Well, now,' said Quinlan, 'if we'd known you were plannin' on giving us the pleasure of your company we wouldn't have gone to such trouble to find you ourselves.'

'Happy to oblige,' snarled Herne through his teeth. 'Now take me to your boss and remember that if you try any tricks on the way, this gun isn't going to miss.'

Quinlan winked and led the way across the main gaming room towards Daniels' office. They were on the stairs below the roulette wheel when the office door opened and Daniels came out. He looked a lot less worried than he might have done. His eyes were steady as he gazed down at Herne and there wasn't a crease in his dark suit or a scuff mark on his shoes. A tie pin glistened on his chest. He looked like a man who'd just won ten thousand dollars and knew that that was only the beginning.

'Mister Herne, who'd have thought you'd have come back so soon – and of your own accord?'

'Never mind the smart talk, Daniels. You won't be looking so cool and pleased with yourself when you've heard what I've got to say.'

'Really, Mister Herne? Well, if you insist. Although if I

were in your shoes I wouldn't be so confident.'

Herne gestured to Quinlan to continue up the stairs and stand at the far side of the roulette table. Daniels watched with an amused detachment which was getting Herne worried. The gambler had more than aces up his sleeve and as yet Herne didn't know what.

Then he did.

She came out of the office, a drink in her hand, a cigarette posed at the corner of her mouth. Veronica Russell was wearing a lime green gown that her dressmaker had sewn onto her body just before she left the house. Her dark hair was swept up in a chignon and held in place with a diamond clip in the shape of a moon.

She looked very beautiful and very dangerous.

'Veronica here has a story to tell, don't you, my dear? How you came back to the Russell house in the middle of the night with blood on your hands and clothes and her younger sister drugged and helpless in your care. How you told her you'd broken into Ray Bellour's house because of your infatuation with Cassie, quarelled with Bellour and slashed his throat with a broken bottle.'

Herne didn't know whether to laugh aloud at the absurdity of the story, or simply shout Daniels down. But then he looked into the dark of Veronica's eyes and something that he thought he saw there chilled him. If she told that story to the law and he only had his own word to stand against her, who were they likely to believe . . . ?

Daniels hadn't finished. 'The policeman in charge of the case is a man named Wallace. He's good at his work. He doesn't like stray ends. He's also a good friend of mine. How else do you think I keep this place open without being raided and my customers harassed? Wallace does well out of me – very well. If I hand him Bellour's killer all neatly tied up, he'll have the rope round your neck so fast it's doubtful you'll know what's happening.'

He laughed his smug, self-satisfied laugh. 'But then, cowboy, you don't really know what's happening here anyway, do you? You should have stayed out west with your cattle rustlers and stage robbers and simple things you can handle.'

He laughed again and walked the short distance to Veronica and took hold of her hand, squeezing it as he kissed the side of her neck.

Herne looked for a sign of distaste in her eyes but saw nothing.

Quinlan giggled and gave a little clap with his hands.

'You're forgetting one thing, Daniels. I know this laughing fool here and that mountain you keep around were the ones who carried Bellour's body out of the house and dumped him in the bay.'

'Really?' Daniels raised an eyebrow. 'And can you prove that?'

'With witnesses. Two of them.'

Daniels shook his head. 'I wonder who'd believe them. But even if the court thought it true, what would it prove? Disposing of a body is not the same thing as murder. Unless these witnesses of yours saw that too . . . ?'

Herne opened his mouth to say something, but the words failed to come. He knew that he was having the floor pulled out from underneath him; he knew that if Veronica would swear that he'd admitted to killing Bellour everything was going to stand against him. He was the outsider, the man who'd stuck his head where it wasn't wanted and didn't belong — stuck his head into the dark and now they were going to drop a noose about it and pull it tight.

They . . .

Daniels, Quinlan, even the dead Bellour . . . even Veronica.

He wondered how long it would be before the law arrived and his chances of getting out of San Francisco were more or less blocked out. But he still had the Colt in his hand and there was no one preventing him from turning round and going back through the same door he'd entered.

Except that he didn't like what was happening to him; he didn't like the frame he was being trapped inside; he didn't like what that too-perfect looking woman was doing to him. That woman who . . .

He stared at her and remembered the shape of her breasts

against his body, the softness of her mouth and the twisting of her tongue.

Daniels leered at her green-encased body and for a second his tongue appeared between his fleshy lips.

'Have you told her about the money you were trying to get from her father, Daniels?' Herne said angrily, moving a couple of treads up the stairs. 'Have you told her about that?'

Daniels moved away from Veronica and flashed him a warning look but Herne wasn't about to be warned.

'Tell her how you tried to get a couple of thousand dollars from a dying man.'

Veronica was looking at him now, those dark eyes staring at the gambler's fleshy face.

'You said they were gambling debts, but that wasn't the truth. The major didn't believe that, but he didn't know the truth. Part of him didn't want to know but the rest of him couldn't stomach getting drawn into the kind of rottenness that you and your kind live their lives in. That was why he sent for me. To lean on you, stop you if I could . . . and if not throw things out into the open, get it over somehow, some way.

'He's a brave old man and no matter how far his bones have decayed he's still got more spine that you've ever had. You don't need backbone to blackmail a dying old man. And that's what it was, wasn't it. Blackmail.'

Herne was slowly going forward, his eyes fixed on Daniels, waiting for him to make some kind of a move.

'If he paid up regardless, then so much the better. You'd count your money and laugh about it and then there'd be another note and then another. And if he didn't pay, you'd send him one of Bellour's nice little pictures. Cassie in a little girl's frock, playing on a swing. Cassie in her crib. Cassie dressed up in her wedding veil.'

'You're insane, Herne! You're babbling! There isn't any truth in what you're say . . .'

Herne squeezed back on the trigger of the Colt and the roulette wheel jumped and spun.

Daniels jumped backwards, one pudgy hand moving too

slowly towards his coat pocket.

Herne fired again and this time the slug embedded itself into the wall less than a foot to the right of the gambler's head.

'You best tell the truth, Daniels. Tell Veronica. Let her hear it. Tell her about the notes you sent the major. Tell her!'

Herne stopped walking and aimed the .45 at Daniels' heart.

The gambler's mouth dropped open and both hands swung forward, palms outward, begging Herne not to shoot.

'Tell her!'

'I thought . . . I wanted . . . Hell, he's got so much money he doesn't know what to do with it. He's not going to miss a couple of thousand, is he?

Daniels was looking at Veronica, his head turned towards her, his voice more and more imploring. She continued to stare back at him, through him. It was impossible to tell what she was thinking; if she was thinking at all.

Herne waited for her to say something, react.

Finally she swished the green gown as she moved a pace towards Herne and said: 'Is that all you've got to say, cowboy?'

Quinlan laughed his high-pitched laugh and rubbed his hands with glee.

Daniels stopped sweating and a glint came back to his eyes. 'You're out on a limb, Herne. Right out on the end and here comes the man who's going to saw it right off.'

Daniels was looking past Herne, down towards the main room.

Herne swung his head for an instant, expecting to see the policeman with the bowler hat and the plaid coat. At first he saw no one and then, bulking against the curtain by the door there was the Chinaman.

Quinlan rushed him.

Herne spun fast and the barrel of the Colt caught the Irishman on the side of the jaw and swung him round. Quinlan fell awkwardly, cannoning off the roulette table and back against Herne's legs. A fist drove hard into Herne's groin. His eyes watered and he doubled forward. The little man's head smacked into his nose and blood spurted freely.

The steps close at his back shook with the weight of the running man.

Again Herne tried to turn, but the Irishman was clinging to his legs as if his life depended upon it. A fist the size of a man's head slammed against Herne's ear and he couldn't prevent himself from falling. The back of his skull struck the thick leg of the roulette table and colours exploded and faded fast at the back of his eyelids.

Something metallic slammed hard against his temple and the colours turned to black, the black became a tunnel and he fell down it.

His head felt as if it had been on the receiving end of a charge from a five hundred pound bull. At least one of the wounds from the last time Daniels' men had worked him over had opened up again. He could feel the dried blood that had coiled around his ear and down the side of his neck. He could feel the tightness of the ropes that kept his arms tight at his back, his ankles locked against one another.

Someone was singing off-key deep inside his brain.

Gradually words seeped through the pain of the song. Voices he recognised as belonging to Daniels and Veronica. They were in the room next to his and the door was ajar. Herne figured they'd carried him upstairs out of the way. There was a bed over to the side of the room and through the slit in the door he could see an armchair, a leg lightly swinging, the top of it encased in lime green. The smell of cigarette smoke and good bourbon.

The song stopped shrieking enough for him to hear what was being said.

' . . . sort of deal did you and Bellour have figured out?' It was Veronica's voice, relaxed, almost warm, a deep purr.

'He needed contacts to sell his merchandise. He met them through me. Here. I put him in touch with people and in exchange he gave me a cut. Twenty per cent.'

'You're a shrewd man, Cord,' she said admiringly.

'I try to be.'

There was a clink of glass against glass, the spurt and hiss of a match. Herne tried to ease his wrists inside the rope but it was useless.

'How about girls, Cord?' Veronica asked. 'Did he meet any of those here?'

A pause. Then: 'One or two. Once in a while, I'd introduce him to someone pretty, young. The kind he liked.'

'Cassie?'

The pause was longer. 'Cassie? He may have met her here, I don't know.'

Veronica laughed and the sound chilled Herne, whatever effect it had on Daniels. 'Relax, Cord, you know there's no love lost between Cassie and myself. She's always run wild. That's the way she is.'

Daniels chuckled. 'You're right. She's wild okay. According to Ray, once she got going there wasn't any stopping her. Why, she had ideas that even *he* hadn't thought of.'

He laughed some more and the glass clinked again as the decanter poured out the last of the bourbon. There was a sound that was unmistakably that of two people kissing.

A few moments later there was Veronica's deep voice again. 'You're a clever man, Cord. You introduced Bellour to his clients and his girls which meant you had both of them at your mercy.'

'What do you mean, Veronica?'

'I mean, Cord, my dear, that in the fullness of time you were in the position to blackmail the whole damn lot of them!'

The laughter of the couple merged together and only faltered when Daniels stood up. 'I guess I've been drinking too much. I don't know how you women hold it like you do. I'll be right back.'

His laugh was shut off by the closing of a door.

Herne looked up and Veronica was standing there in the

doorway. This time there was no doubting what was in her eyes. The hate itself was almost enough to burn through his ropes.

'Inside my right boot,' he said urgently, 'there's a bayonet. You can . . .'

She put a finger to her lips, silencing him. When she knelt beside him, he could feel the warmth and slight trembling of her body. The bayonet slid from the boot into her hands and she began to saw at the rope at his back.

In the other room the door opened and steps came close across the carpet.

'Be quick!' Herne hissed.

She was not quite through the first strand when Daniels came through the doorway. It took him a moment to realise what was happening and as soon as he did his face went white and he fumbled inside his pocket for the derringer he carried there.

Veronica stood up and faced him. The bayonet was still in her hand and there was less than four yards between them.

'You do a very good job of changing sides,' snarled Daniels.

The derringer was tight in his fist and the skin between the knuckles was stretched taut and white. His face was flushed now with anger, its pallor disappeared.

'You realise, Veronica, you have just thrown away a great deal.' He raised an eyebrow and looked pityingly at Herne. 'And why? For that simple-minded cowboy?' He threw back his head and laughed and at that moment Veronica started to walk towards him.

'Veronica, don't be stupid!'

The blade of the bayonet was thrust out before her, lifting higher the closer she got.

'Don't!'

Sweat swung from Daniels' brow as he took a half step back against the door frame and fired.

The .22 slug tore at the green of Veronica's arm, plucked at the skin. Blood bubbled out and down, dark on the green.

Not for a second did she stop staring at him. Quite still now. Watching.

Daniels waited for her to fall, drop the bayonet, run.

Instead she went forward.

The gambler lifted the derringer, sweat running down into his eyes, his hand beginning to shake. He willed himself to use the gun a second time but his finger refused to move.

Veronica's eyes held him trapped, sweating, gibbering, terrified.

When the blade pushed against his heart he opened his mouth to scream. Veronica clutched the end of the bayonet with both hands, leaned her weight against it, pushed some more, twisted, and was done.

She stepped back and watched as Cord Daniels shivered against the door and his body began slowly to sink towards the floor.

A thin trickle of blood ran from his still open mouth.

Sounds gargled out, wordless, without meaning.

Veronica continued to gaze at the lengthening line of blood, at the way his shirt darkened around the blade, the twitch of his hands and the irregular drumming of his feet.

'That's for Cassie, you bastard!'

Her hands tightened back around the bayonet and she heaved it clear. Blood followed heavily in its wake. She didn't stop to wipe the blade clean before using it to cut the rest of Herne's bonds.

As the final one was severed, the body of Cord Daniels fell sideways onto the floor, his face wedged against the carpet, and didn't move again.

Chapter Twelve

Herne rubbed at his ankles and wrists and tried to get the circulation going as quick as he could. His head throbbed constantly and each fresh movement sent a hammer blow juddering through it.

Footsteps were coming up the stairs fast.

The door to the far room was flung back and the big Chinaman came barrelling through, Herne's Colt .45 in one hand and a massive club dangling from the other.

He yelled something undecipherable and ran half way across the room.

The sight of Cord Daniel's sprawled, dead body brought him up short.

Herne moved fast, snatching the blade from the carpet where Veronica had left it. His body swung through a low crouch and his right arm extended backwards, the vicious looking blade at the end of it. When the arm swung back, angling up, all that was visible was a dark blur with a silver tip. The bayonet left Herne's hand at a speed that was too fast to pick out.

Its trajectory took it curving wickedly upwards towards the Chinaman's chest and vainly he clawed his hands towards it. His left hand touched it as it sped past and his little finger sheered away. Nothing could prevent the point breaking the flesh above the chest bone and deflecting upwards off the edge of the bone and burying itself below the Adam's apple.

The giant of a man swayed on his heels, rocked forward onto his toes. Six inches of the blade had disappeared from sight. His fingers sought the end of the weapon and strove to drag it free.

Herne went forward fast, snaked out his boot and kicked

the Colt clear.

It was in his hand when Quinlan's amazed face peered round the edge of the far door.

'Mary, mother of God!' he sighed and crossed himself.

Herne covered him with the gun.

The Chinaman finally succeeded in wrenching the bayonet from his throat and the effort sent him down against the floor with a thud that shook the boards. He groaned and rolled over onto his back, his face already a vivid mask of blood. His tongue rolled, his hands stretched up towards Herne and he kicked out with his boots, anything to strike out at the man who had killed him.

'Get in here, Quinlan!'

The Irishman wasn't about to refuse. He came with his hands as far towards the ceiling as he could, paused when he saw Veronica at Herne's back, nodded in sudden understanding and waited to do as he was told.

'Get that gun he carries with him,' said Herne, speaking to Veronica without looking round. 'Then use that rope to tie him up.' He glanced at the huge figure struggling amidst his own blood on the ground. 'We'll take him below first. The law can clear up the rest of this mess up here.'

Quinlan's gun in her hand she looked at him, hesitant. 'The law . . . ?'

'He came at you with a pistol, fired a shot. You've the wound in your arm to prove it. You didn't have any choice.' He looked back at the gambler's still body. 'Besides, Wallace won't be getting any more from Daniels. He's got no reason to protect him.'

Herne gestured with the Colt and the Irishman walked dejectedly down the stairs, doubtless rehearsing his story so as to come out of it as innocent as possible.

At the foot of the staircase, Veronica turned against him and her body was not quite still beneath the closeness of her dress. Her skin shimmered with sweat. For the first time he could smell her more strongly than the perfume she wore. He liked it. Her face was inches away from his.

'You were good,' he said quietly. 'You had me worried for a long while, but you were very damn good.'

Her kiss was as he remembered it: now and much later. 'You were pretty good yourself.'

Major Russell insisted on pouring the brandy himself, although it was necessary for Lucas to push the wheelchair around the room so that he could hand a glass to Herne and both of his daughters.

Cassie was looking pale and weak and her eyes seemed hollow, seeing little if anything that passed in front of her. Each time she moved, Lucas swung his head towards her in panic, as if thinking she might fall.

As for Veronica, she seemed to have been through no more than a hard night watching the roulette wheel spin the ball away from her personal number. She was wearing white and she looked like she'd just stepped out of a pack of ice from down on the dock. Once, she looked across the room and gave him a conspiratorial smile, but that was all. It was almost as if nothing of the last few days had happened; everything had slipped from sight beneath one of those sea fogs that came rolling up out of the bay.

'You did a damn fine job, Mister Herne,' said the Major, lifting his glass towards him. 'If it hadn't been for you Daniels would have been bleeding what little life I've got left out of me and taking countless others for what he could get into the bargain. As for Bellour . . .' His eyes passed over Cassie's slight, childlike body and a shudder passed over his aging heart. 'Men like him are best not born — born, they're better dead.'

He nodded towards Lucas and grudgingly Lucas picked up a long envelope from the sideboard and came forward to Herne with it in his hands.

'There's a bonus there, Mister Herne, for a job well done. I thank you, sir, with all my heart.'

'Fine, major. Only it ain't finished. Quite.'

Lucas stopped in front of him and their eyes met and held.

'Daniels didn't kill Bellour. His men didn't either. He wanted the body out of the way to stop the law poking too close into his business. Maybe there's still one or two of 'em he didn't have in his pocket. But he didn't kill him . . . not Connors either.'

Lucas was staring at him hard, his breathing becoming loud and laboured.

'Whoever killed Connors did it out of jealousy. He was getting good looks from Cassie an' I'd guess a whole lot more. Connors was looking after her in ways you weren't exactly payin' him for that didn't go down well. Did it, Lucas?

'As for Bellour, when you followed Cassie to his house and found out what was going on there wasn't any way he was goin' to get out alive.'

He took a pace towards Lucas and only stopped when he could feel the warm, stuttering breath on his face.

'You killed 'em for good reasons, maybe, the way you saw it. You killed 'em for Cassie's sake an' Bellour, anyway, had it comin'. After what I saw I'd likely have killed him myself. But whichever way you look at it, you killed 'em both.'

Lucas froze for a moment and then swung his fist towards Herne's face. Herne, waiting for the blow, swayed and blocked and at the same time his hand sped to the Colt .45 at his hip.

Before Lucas could throw another punch the end of the barrel was resting tight against his chest, hard under the heart.

The major stared in sorrow at the man who had served him so well for so many years. Cassie rocked backwards and forwards on her heels, her sobs growing as she realised her part in what had happened.

Herne glanced across towards Veronica. 'If you open the door, you should find that policeman, Wallace, outside. He'll take over from here.'

She looked at him for a moment with something approaching admiration, then left the room.

She didn't speak to him again.

The major did his best to persuade Herne to stay at the house for a spell longer but he'd seen all he wanted to of the city and knew that he wouldn't breathe right until he was clear in open country once again.

He did see her, a fleeting image when he turned at the end of the drive. A dark-haired figure in white at the bay window above the door, there for a moment and then gone, blocked from sight as the shutter was pulled across.

When the image came back to him — as it sometimes would, nights alone in a rented bed or on hard ground under the moon — it was never real, but something he had seen in a painting, glimpsed in some strange restless dream. He knew that if he ever reached out and tried to touch it, his fingers would pass through cold air and the image would fade: and knowing that, he was glad.

THE END

HERNE THE HUNTER 20 – HEARTS OF GOLD
by John J. McLaglen

Five men stood around a young woman, sinking their boots into her body, striking her with their fists, shouting and spitting at her. The lank-haired stranger burst amongst them, hauling off the nearest pair and pistol-whipping a third to his knees. He ducked beneath a fist and sank his own into one man's overfed belly. A boot struck him in the back of the thigh and he turned fast, slashing out with his gun barrel and breaking half a dozen teeth in the attacker's mouth . . . They fled as best they could . . .

Jed Herne came to the rescue of Mary Anne Marie and her girls whilst on the trail of a gang of bank robbers who'd been posing as a minister and his two sons.

Madam Mary Ann Marie offered Jed the job of bodyguard to her five 'soiled doves' and – able to combine this new post with trailing the gang – Herne accepted.

0 552 12070 7   95p

HERNE THE HUNTER 21 – PONY EXPRESS
by John J. McLaglen

Herne aimed for the boy's chest, near the throat. That way the fifty-five ball would certainly hit something. Probably heart and lungs. Maybe the spine. If it went high it was through the throat. Low and it opened up the target's belly. A hand's breadth to either side and you still had a stopping shot that would kick a grown man to the dirt, eyes blank, looking up at the sky . . . Herne held his breath, shooting two-eyed like all great marksmen. Squeezing the trigger . . .

Jed Herne, riding the vengeance trail, is hunting down Charley Howell, a former galloper with the Pony Express – the lengendary mail service that had turned Jed from a callow boy into a man. Charley and Kid, a cold-eyed teenage killer, had raped and murdered a banker's daughter in Wyoming. And Jed was out to get them both for her brutal and blood-soaked death . . .

0 552 12209 2   95p

A SELECTED LIST
OF CORGI WESTERNS

While every effort is made to keep prices low, it is sometimes necessary to increase prices at short notice. Corgi Books reserve the right to show new retail prices on covers which may differ from those previously advertised in the text or elsewhere.

The prices shown below were correct at the time of going to press.

JOHN J. McLAGLEN
□	**10789 1**	Herne the Hunter 1: White Death	60p
□	**10526 0**	Herne the Hunter 5: Apache Squaw	65p
□	**10720 4**	Herne the Hunter 7: Death Rites	60p
□	**10834 0**	Herne the Hunter 9: Massacre!	65p
□	**11130 9**	Herne the Hunter 11: Silver Threads	75p
□	**11312 3**	Herne the Hunter 13: Billy the kid	85p
□	**11585 1**	Herne the Hunter 15: Till Death	85p
□	**11689 0**	Herne the Hunter 16: Geronimo	95p
□	**11892 3**	Herne the Hunter 18: Dying Ways	95p
□	**11990 3**	Herne the Hunter 19: Blood Line	95p
□	**12070 7**	Herne the Hunter 20: Hearts of Gold	95p

JAMES W. MARVIN
□	**11461 8**	Crow 4: The Black Trail	85p
□	**12011 1**	Crow 8: A Good Day	£1.00

OLIVER STRANGE
□	**11795 1**	Sudden: Marshal of Lawless	95p
□	**11796 X**	Sudden Outlawed	95p
□	**11797 8**	Sudden	95p
□	**11798 6**	Sudden Plays A Hand	95p

FREDERICK H. CHRISTIAN
□	**11799 4**	Sudden At Bay	95p
□	**11800 1**	Sudden, Apache Fighte	95p

All these books are available at your book shop or newsagent, or can be ordered direct from the publisher. Just tick the titles you want and fill in the form below.

CORGI BOOKS, Cash Sales Department, P.O. Box 11, Falmouth, Cornwall.

Please send cheque or postal order, no currency.

Please allow cost of book(s) plus the following for postage and packing:

U.K. Customers—Allow 45p for the first book, 20p for the second book and 14p for each additional book ordered, to a maximum charge of £1.63.

B.F.P.O. and Eire—Allow 45p for the first book, 20p for the second book plus 14p per copy for the next 7 books, thereafter 8p per book.

Overseas Customers—Allow 75p for the first book and 21p per copy for each additional book.

NAME (Block Letters) ....

ADDRESS ....

....